A Future's Dream

GCM

Published by GCM, 2025.

This is a work of fiction. Similarities to real people, places, or events are entirely coincidental.

A FUTURE'S DREAM

First edition. July 7, 2025.

ISBN: 979-8231821198

Written by GCM.

Dedicated to the people who's survival is why I'm here today and those who will prosper from my existence in the future.

I thank you all!

<u>GCM</u>

Foreword

It's sad that humanity still suffers greed. As my son once said to me,

'Humans are the only species that pay to live on this planet.'

This isn't a biography about the importance of one's existence.

The are no facts or truth contained here and all content and beliefs are nothing further than a fabrication.

Ego to ascension perhaps?

If enough people believe a lie does it become a truth?

A belief to realise a future for our species' evolution is all that resides here...

Be entertained, be inspired.

Menu

In a dream one must be allowed the liberty of imagining occasionally that which never existed in the world of sense perception. - Joseph Kepler

'I have a dream...' Martin Luther King once said to me. Well he's not the only one. The problem with dreams is they can get you killed. For mine is beyond a dream. It is my curse. I will save our species against the otherwise inevitable. As if within a Mayan premonition, I believe I am the chosen one.

Ask not what your species can do for you, ask what you can do for your species.

And you may ask why do you need me? Well let me crudely divulge.

The Earth is 4.5 billion years old. It has taken us 5 million years to evolve to where we are today. And if nothing else happens, the sun might give us a billion more. However, I envisage we will be lucky to last a couple of hundred. Either due to our own fault as addicts to greed and ignorance or external influences to our planet and being subject to an accelerating expanding universe. Perhaps our ancestors thought the same?

But before we examine the cure then let me explain who I am and my epiphany.

1.

My Epiphany.

May I ask? Have you ever considered what was the defining moment in your existence? Can you remember when you drew your first breath? Opened your eyes? Took your first steps?

Made your first creation and affected the world that surrounds you? When did you become self-aware? When did you have an understanding of your survival needs and when did you challenge its hurdles, threats and boundaries? Was there a defining point? An inciting incident? Was it one or all of your existing moments acting as cognitive and inspirational awareness? When did you consider yourself old and of no further aid to your species?

Some believe the future is just as defined as the present becoming the past. So are we really destined? If it already exists then there is only the inevitability of becoming that which has already happened. Perhaps time is someone else's concept?

So where is our moment defined I ask?

Imagine if it was 1969. The day of the Apollo Moon launch and me waking in Mexico City soaked in a puddle of piss with a 5 dollar harlot during the Day of the Dead. This would be apt for my defining moment. Where I thought about our ancestors and what we owed them and our future lineage. However this would simply be a lie but a dramatic start to my story none-the-less and the legends that maketh yours.

It would also be cool to say my father was a mercenary and my mother a prostitute (Here's to you Galileo!), although this wasn't uncommon for the time. However this too would remain untrue.

My defining moment, my equilibrium began elsewhere.

The truth is I had an abnormally normal upbringing. I wasn't an orphan from a war torn country, neither a product of 2 cousins marrying or a genetic experiment escaped from the lab. My parents loved one another and never argued. They both worked 9-5 jobs and we lived in suburbia. Surrounded by 2.2

families living life as utopians. Birth, jobs, marriage, retirement and death. A lovely design of life. Simple and unassuming. Something trying to emanate 1950's American suburban utopia. Like David Lynch meets Dennis Potter. Absurdly normal with an underlying world kept locked away from prying eyes.

One of my earliest memories I can recall was as a boy of schooling age. It was a clear winter's late afternoon with the dark drawing in like a high tide. A light breeze brought a chill to the air. School had ended and I was eager to get home so I took a short cut through the woods and the fields. Reaching a fast running stream, I crossed the stepping stones to get back before the start of my favourite TV programme. Half way across I felt an urge to stop and gaze up to the heavens. And it was here where they appeared before me. I felt as if time before and consequently thereafter was irrelevant. Three blue neutron stars burning in an inverse triangle set against the background of darkness as if from a Van Goth painting.

Was this the cosmos calling? Is light life?

That night I dreamt of a highly distraught woman screaming as her baby was taken from her by the authorities.

Up to this point all was pretty much the same as many others that surrounded me.

I would later spend many an evening staring up into the night's sky, attempting to ascertain whether I was the subject of a vision, a visit or simply part of a dream.

I often visualized the planets ferociously swirling around distant stars without noise. And mixed with for some reason, the image of the 1980's Hollywood stunt man, Mad Mike

Hughes as he climbed into his self made rocket launching himself on his fateful last journey.

I asked myself thus:

'It has been discovered that for every star there is at least one planet orbiting it. It has also been proven that one person can build their own rocket and leave the Earth's crust. I do not consider myself a genius for I stand upon the shoulders of giants before me. To exist is an honour. To evolve is a duty.' So why does the majority of our species wish to remain wilfully blinkered?

I remember looking across to my father as I released a helium balloon, watching it drift away with the song in my mind, 'Who wants to live forever.' Performed operatically by Freddie Mercury & Queen.

Can you imagine the floods, famine and wars all of which avoidable if we possessed the greater concept of cause and causality? All seemed somewhat distant through the eyes of the television and yet standing upon our door step banging to gain entry. Imagine outside of this an asteroid hurtling towards us with the concept of the unavoidable. There are more of us now. That's 8 billion beautiful brains. Outside of necessity, imagine what our species has the potential to accomplish!

Can we avoid a car crash?

During an ancient Mayan ceremony, did a shaman look up upon the night's sky and witness the same sign as I? The three burning blue stars aligning to beam a single light upon him?

Like an apple falling upon Newton's head (which is apparently incorrect), many have claimed their eureka moment to be a coincidence of events. Mine however is the culmination of past events indicating no other option, perhaps funnelling to pursue my destiny. A singularity. For when I look back, fate has been my master.

But despite my calling, I am haunted with the vision of a hysterical drug addict teenager who's baby is placed into a basket and left upon the church door. Well this seems more poetic than a child being snatched out of her distraught arms from the authorities.

The sun was shining, the air was crisp and I was sporting my Sunday Best as I walked down the stairs and out to the car to join Mum and Dad for our weekly ritual oppression. The Church! And as we drove off, I swear Galileo and Copernicus were waving at me.

I paraphrase,

'The Catholic Church is nothing like the Nazis, we don't dress in black and tell people what to do with their lives.' Thanks Father Ted Crilley.

The Church yes, where not only were you spoon feed concepts that were simply alien to me, it felt we were being press ganged into another man's philosophies through praise and song. Indoctrinated? Threatened? Oh yes...

However as I sat I noticed the light piecing the idyllic stain glass window depicting Moses on the Mount. Was he reaching out to me? It was at this point that despite my destain, my joy was to sing louder than the congregation to a point of distraction causing an unnecessary concern for my parents.

'All things bright and beautiful!'

Mum tried to shhh me!

'Each flower that opens!' Isn't this the point of worship?

'Each little bird that sings!' Or perhaps delusion?

'...he made their glowing colours, he made their tiny wings!'

'Jason! Your causing a scene!' Mum cursed.

Maybe hope? I was never designed to fit in.

I took heed of mum. But as I looked up to witness the unimpressed faces of the old, who were maybe there searching for answers to their existences and for their future saviour beyond this world, there she was! A Goth girl in the choir smirking at me. Goth I ask? Was this a statement sporting or taunting the afterlife? Perhaps this Angel of Heaven has a sense of humour after all.

Following Sunday School we would often take a walk through the park to admire all that was bright and beautiful! The trees, the spring daffodils, the homeless tramp and the hooded gang of drug dealers. My parents normally shunned away from Speakers Corner however on this particular occasion they stopped on seeing a man who looked like the 11th Doctor, Matt Smith dressed rather dramatically in a monks robes preaching to the dwindling the lesser masses.

'Everything you think is important is irrelevant. Your wars, your protests, your petty beliefs, your very existences whilst you choose to be distracted. Your lives are not your own! Open your eyes and then you will see!'

'Is he a Jehovah's Witness?' Asked my mum. My father looked somewhat elsewhere. And yet Matt Smith or his doppelgänger heard!

'No dear lady, I'm a physicist!'

My mum seemed unimpressed and we left him to his further rants at the heavens, being there was a lack of his followers.

However his words stuck with me in light of the world that surrounds us.

Are we living in delusion? Are we being kept in delusion? What is the real point of focus? And why don't we care? I ask myself.

2.

I am the Chosen One!

Is there a fine line between education and propaganda?

Sat in the front row of Sunday School the Vicar towered above us.

'Does anyone know the story of Moses and the Exodus?'

Breaking the silence a boy bravely extended his hand.

'Didn't he build the Ark?'

'That's Noah. But the story of Moses is the story of how one man led the slaves from persecution to freedom.'

It was at this point I too held my hand aloft.

'Yes Jason?'

'I need the toilet.'

And being waved off now desperate to avoid a trouser accident, I discovered the relief parlour was otherwise occupied. So using my sense of ingenuity the Fire Escape beckoned. Finding a secluded spot my relief was satisfied even though my conscience felt somewhat anarchistic by urinating upon the religious house of reflection and solitude. I can assure you, it was no disrespect only necessity.

'I like your statement' A soft voice called out.

With both shock and embarrassment I managed to secure my man chipolata back in its housing, turning to see her smoking a fag.

'What, uh I'm sorry?'

'Against our oppressors.'

'I don't know what you mean.' I hastily replied.

'Here, the government, the authority, you know.' She blows smoke into my face. Was she the Devil recruiting?

'Uh, sorry. Someone was using the toilet. Why are you smoking?' I asked this rebellious femme fatal.

'Because I can. Would you like to try?'

Shaking my head with confusion, 'Who are you?'

And with a fiendish smile that would melt a choir boy's innocents, 'Mary. The Vicar's daughter.' How could I deny her worldly charms? I took her cigarette and attempting to impress her with a drag however there can be nothing less cool than a boy coughing his guts up! With that the Fire Escape door flung open. Our tyrant had been summoned!

'What in heavens are you doing boy! Wait until your parents hear about this! Get inside!'

With one swift move the Vicar grabbed the cigarette from my hand stubbing it out on the floor and led me back inside by my ear (Very Old Testament!). I remember glancing back at Mary thinking I too could be easily influenced as I was suffering a tingly feeling. I wondered whether this is love?

I believe everything is an influence that has led me to be your saviour. Even the smaller points such as the ritual Sunday Roast!

And there I was shovelling food down my chops whilst in quiet contemplation. Mum was slicing her beef like it had insulted her.

'More peas Jason? Greens will make you big and strong. Like me.' Dad said with a generous smile.

'Dad, why hasn't Mum been talking?'

'Mum's just a little upset.'

'It wasn't my fault. She made me do it'

Mum slapped her knife and fork down onto the table.

'Upset! I'm very disappointed. Have you any idea what I've been through to bring you into this world?! And you want to destroy yourself smoking those disgusting sticks of filth. How dare you! You are being judged!'

I tried to respond without further upset to her, 'I thought we are all the Lord's,'

'FXXk the Lord!'

I've never witnessed Mum like this before and even Dad was left speechless.

'You are like my flesh and blood. Did the Lord put food on the table, clothe you, stay up all night when you were sick? No! I did! And you do this to me?!'

Apart from the outburst something seemed odd, 'like?' Dad was always the assigned peacemaker.

'Martha! Please. He made a mistake and learned from it. Now lets all settle down.'

'And think about our reputation. Our son, the drug addict!' Up to this point Mum has always been a stranger to emotion. She stormed out crying, thundering up the stairs to her bedroom. And like a thunder clap her door slammed shut.

'It's OK Jason, Mum's just a tad distracted at the moment.'

'Why? I don't understand.'

'Lets just say, you might not be a lonely child for long.'

'Dad? Why do Mum's have babies?' I was asking with a greater philosophy in mind as he spooned more peas unto my plate.

What was the lesson here I ask. Lineage? The demanded survival of the gene? 'You are 'like my flesh and blood' Am I the boy in the basket? Was this part education?

Whilst the other kids played games such as Leap Frog and Trip Up British Bull Dogs I would often sit in a quieter area of the school playground indulging in my research. On this particular occasion, Darwin had the honour of my attention with 'The Origin of Species.' I only had to look up to understand his theories with the Neanderthal organisms that surrounded me. However this is probably not the way I should view my fellow students! After-all, was I beyond them and everything they ever hoped to be. My visions looked beyond the school fence and funny enough as I did so there she was. Mary with her entourage of male friends on their daily escapades. As she pasted, she glanced back with a smile and a cheeky wave. I could have melted if not saved by the break time bell. I didn't know it was possible to become distracted or driven my emotional responses.

Although Biology was a deeply intriguing subject my teacher, Mr Moreau didn't wholly inspire interest. When you look back at your school years they say you only remember the teachers who had character. My imagination had to fill in the blanks as I envisaged he had escaped from an island where HG Wells had kept him prisoner for genetic experimentation.

'Class, who can tell me the different ways an organism can reproduce?' He asked in a rather droll mannered voice. Surprisingly hands were raised!

'Fish, reptiles and birds lays eggs',

'Mammals give birth.' And quite unexpectedly a rather large figured girl in the back of the room replied,

'The mushroom worm, through cloning sir.' Was there something hidden in the school dinners today? Why were they expressing both knowledge and interest when I was elsewhere for a change.

'And you Jason?' He called.

'What sir?'

'Have you been paying any attention? The answer is not outside the window.'

I wasn't trying to be arrogant when I answered, 'Mitosis or Meiosis.' I only wished to dismiss his focus from me as I was otherwise deep in thought without the a distraction breaking my distant concentration. Mr Moreau seemed somewhat confused as I operated outside of the structured text books.

'How can an organism reproduce, Jason? What? Where did you hear about that?'

'All the answers are outside.' Perhaps I embarrassed his authority within the class.

'Jason, see me after class.' I hasten to ask, but perhaps I too was subject to distraction as unfortunately school was the last this on my mind. I only wanted to see her again. For she is my kindred spirit, my guiding angel, my Mary Magdalene and destiny dictates such.

Despite sports being a subject I was far intellectually removed from, looking back at it there was a lesson to be learned. Supporting always confused me. It seemed futile that you should follow a team who knew not of your existence even though worshipping them as your own or the fact of shouting at a telly in the vain hope a referee can heed your mighty words of wisdom. I felt football at school was no different. Which is why I was always picked last and pushed into goal. Even the fat kids were of more appeal than I. It did however provide an opportunity of deep contemplation. It wasn't uncommon for the opposing team to rejoice at how easy it became to shoot the ball past me!

'Open goal! Jason! What are you doing?!' The fat defender would commonly shout followed by 'You twat! Why didn't you save it?!' To which I would reply,

'Why? What is the point?'

The after game talk was always interesting with words of encouragement from the coach.

'You little shit! You lost us the game. Open goal? You had nothing to loose! Why? Why didn't you make an effort? It's not just about you!'

'I had a moment of clarity Coach.'

'A moment of what?'

'I lost the point of its importance. A futile effort. That's why no action was utilised.'

'Futile! It's a game of team work and competition. Without competition no-one would strive for anything! Understand! You're off the team!'

He was to say the most passionate about something I wasn't. I thanked him with a smile without meaning to antagonise him further. Maybe he was right. It's not about me.

The following Sunday was Harvest Festival at the church and Mum was holding the head up high despite what she thought others might be thinking. And for a change I was seeing an alternative meaning behind the songs. So I sang with conviction rather than trying to make a statement.

'We plough the fields and scatter the good seed on the land, but it is fed and watered by God's all mighty hand.'

I winked at Mary and gave her my best enthusiastic double thumbs up when Mum wasn't looking. Mary turned away as if I had expended my use. Perhaps she would take me seriously if I looked like Slash from Guns & Roses serenading her with my screaming riffs and pelvic thrusts? Could she picture me leather cladded screaming 'All things bright and beautiful!' emersed with the light piecing through the stained glass windows? Perhaps so?

'Jason! Are you paying attention?' called the Vicar as he slammed his Bible shut. Yes, sat once again in Sunday School and something was plaguing me.

'Yes sir, sorry but I have a question.' He looked somewhat curious.

'I'm interested in Moses. Was he a dictator or a liberator?'

Now confused, 'Sorry?'

'Did the people follow him to save themselves from the wrath of King Herod or did they believe he was the voice of God and had no option? If the leaders considered themselves as shepherds, does this make the followers a herd? The masses being like sheep fearing slaughter or simply mindless?' I think he was impressed with my analytical perceptions. One can't be certain of his thoughts behind that stern countenance.

'I believe you are somewhat confused. It was an escape for their own survival against tyranny.'

Over my shoulder I saw Mary stop in her tracks from collecting books to pay interest. I thought to myself that this guy Moses is someone I could identify with. Was this a turning point? Perhaps one of the greatest stories is of those who free the slaves, leading them to a greater existence?

As all were leaving, my lost angel showed the opposite to what I earlier had come to belief was a lost interest.

'That was brave of you. Where ever did you get such ideas?' She asked with open eyes of intrigue.

'I just get these ideas pop into my head and I didn't see the point in being someone else.'

Perhaps this was my true character beginning to blossom. And with her mischievous smile, 'I can see you're going to be trouble.'

Not quite understanding either her intent or observation but wishing to pursue my sense of reasoning, 'Can I ask you a question?' I cautiously asked. Responding in a playful manor, 'Well the obvious answer would be no.' I couldn't afford the luxury of denial.

'In class the other day, we were studying reproduction...'

'Oh god no. I'm not answering this.'

'Why does anything want to breed?'

And with a surprised pause, 'So life can go on I suppose.'

'Do you want to breed?' Was she taking my questions seriously as I remember her laughs,

'Aren't you a bit young. Someday I might have kids.'

'Is this the point of your existence?'

'Well, is there a point of breeding without ambition? What do you have to pass on? Why exist at all?' I hope I didn't upset her. I think with her father, the vicar re-entering the room gave Mary an excuse from answering my reasoning.

'I'll leave you with King Herod.' She whispering down my ear. The Vicar beckoned me away, 'Jason, come with me. I think we might need to have a quiet discussion with your parents.'

My brain never seemed to be in a state of rest. Like a thousand TV stations all playing at once with constant cross analysis. Is over-thinking a talent or a curse I would often question. There was a time simply whilst submerged within the public at the shops, I would imagine how all that surrounded me was beautifully choreographed as if the subjects of an algorithm. Like the dancers around the Maypole sporting precise precision as if pre-constructed. However there out of the corner of my eye, in the Off-licence was Mary, sneaking a bottle of Vodka into her leather jacket away from the sight of the shop keeper. I don't think she saw me as I continued to observe hid behind a lamppost. Was she making a statement? A rebellion? Was this her thrill or was she simply an alcoholic? With many possibilities, did this fit with the Maypole dance of the others? Maybe it was part of my education to witness behaviour outside of the conventional? Maybe it was because I played witness to Mary's statements I too felt a calling to commit acts outside of the proletariat.

It wasn't unusual to find myself in the library however this time was different. Covertly observing the methodical actions of the librarian I discovered a pattern within her movements to gain a strategy. Once she was distracted by a member of the public, the book which on this occasion beckoned me was by Richard Dawkins, The Selfish Gene, (He was often referred to as Darwin's illegitimate punk offspring). This was to be my mark and an open window being my out point. I could tuck it under my coat and drop it out to be collected later ensuring no funny alarms were triggered upon my exit. This would later become a common act however I wouldn't simply remove these works of genius but I found pleasure maybe even addiction in covertly consuming them. And with gaining higher knowledge that the Greats bestowed came the inevitable, questions. Not about my criminal activities but with their leading purpose and direction.

Covertness was the sport of many when entering an age of awareness. Whilst many would seek the solitude and confinement of the school toilets to examine images of the female form I enjoyed the exclusive privacy of studying the rewards from my criminal activities. I felt sad within our community intelligence is not celebrated. Moreover frowned upon by those who do not wish to attain it or those who feel threatened by it. Therefore it has become a covert activity as I do not wish to be persecuted. However my thirst for knowledge has become more addictive than opium.

In English class my hand stood up proud. 'It's not time for questions Jason.' My teacher would say but I believed otherwise.

'Is the English written language outdated?'

Perhaps it was the system or his withering patience looking to finish this class before the next horde of disinterested plebs arrived. 'Go on. Enlighten us Jason.'

'Well, we only write left to right. How about spherical where concepts like hieroglyphs could be matched on a non linear format? Like a concept helics organically evolving excluding the time constraint? It could resemble a structure like that of DNA strings?' I asked to his tired looking being with the other students seeing me as a mad confused nerd.

In Physics, 'If everything is made up from particles and particles are constructed by the movement and behaviour of energy and energy being the product of friction of space-time or gravity, then is anything real or relevant?' To which the universe's response came from a not so fellow student, 'Geek!'

Biology faired no different, 'If instinct is hereditary, then why can't memory act similarly in DNA coding. Wouldn't it save generations of having to start from scratch with learning the basics? Or, if we are made from the particles that date from the beginning of time, don't we already possess the information of the cosmos and all we need to do is access it? We could awaken that which already resides within us?' There was no response but the obvious 'Nerd!'

And how about history then? 'Why did the Romans fear the Druids? What did they see that we couldn't? With few written texts their gathered knowledge was passed down through their lineage by word of mouth and ceremonies. 'Is this planet doomed for failure Sir?'

'Nob-head!' was quite the usual response received from my piers by now.

Finally I recall in Humanities, 'Is this planet really doomed for failure? Will humans become extinct?' With a spitball hitting the back of my neck answered our pessimistic fate. I could only respond with my angered frustration. 'Like you Benny, it is inevitable that ignorance will become eradicated from history!'

I could no longer tolerate the Vicar's Sunday School lectures whilst my parents wasted their time chatting unimportant pettiness during their coffee morning, so I faked illness to escape this and sat by the church pond. And besides, I don't think he appreciated my questioning his teachings, which is probably closer to the truth. I think he wanted me to re-examine my philosophies outside of the class. Taking a handful of pebbles and throwing them in to observe the consequent expanding ripples I remembered the stars witnessed above. The three inter-twinning ripples were communicating to me. 'Is my destiny calling?' Was my life span enough to make a difference?

Mary made me jump as I turned to see her smoking a cigarette leant against the church wall.

'I said you would be trouble!'

My curiosity got the better of me. 'Are you a virgin?'

Looking surprised at my inquisitive nature, 'You're a funny boy.' She advised in a light hearted condescending manner.

'I believe one day I will need an heir. And if you gave up smoking then your ovaries might be a contender.' Stubbing out her cigarette she laughed.

'Well, mighty sir. I am truly honoured for your graceful request. I'll let you know when my 'ovaries' are free!'

Was the Fire Exit door painted red to symbolise the entrance to hell? It seemed so when the Vicar emerged from it. 'Jason. Your parents are here. Do we need a further discussion?' Was there a point in responding I ask? Well not to him.

'Bye Mary. I hope to see you again soon.'

I could hear him as I left.

'Stay away from that boy. There's something not quite right about him.'

I recall her words,

'Don't we tend to all the members of our flock?'

I recollect my Dad's teachings. It was always subtle but enduring. Did all the Greats ponder whilst consuming an ice-cream looking beyond the horizon with the waves lapping against the shore?

'Dad. What happens when we die?'

'That's a very interesting question which no-one really knows the answer to or have had the opportunity to return to advise us otherwise. What do you think?'

'Nothing. The world turns and we are all but a distant memory.' I replied.

'Well son. That's the scientist in you talking. But the universe could suggest more.'

'So, what happens when you die?'

Answering with a pensive lick of ice-cream he tried to engage my worth.

'Well... You are me. I carry on through you. And your Mum ofcourse.'

Not exactly the illuminating answer I was seeking. Perhaps there is more buried within this simplistic view. Perhaps the greatest philosophers are those who speak in basic terms with a greater meaning underlying? A bit like the Dalai Lama.

'And is that it? What if I don't have a child? What about reincarnation? Energy recreating another form or creating its former self?'

Ever eager to forfill my curiosities Dad widened his point.

'Reincarnation? You see the waves? How they wash against the sand? Well, if we thought about the science lets say, everything leaves a mark on each other. The sand is left wet from the sea and the sea takes away some of the sand. It's all interconnected as you are with the universe.'

'Like this ice-cream? It's me?'

'Precisely. So nothing truly dies it just become something else. Not sure about recreating its former form. However who am I to say.'

And with a smile, there endth that lesson as the sun endeth its sunset. As if suggestive of many philosophies, the sun hasn't left its only moved from our perception.

I often found landscapes were good to gather thoughts so I tried a few eventually finding myself beside the church pond once more during a period of sunset but on this occasion without its direct view only its after-effects. Casting long shadows from the gravestones I felt the dead were trying to reach out returning with the prize of answers stemming from beyond.

'Are you OK Jason? Why are you here?' Being distracted I heard her angelic voice and I looked over my shoulder to see Mary as her father was locking up.

'It just seemed the place to be...' I openly replied.

'It's getting dark. Shouldn't you be home?'

The want of distance was mutual as I felt society was fading from my interest as I walked like a ghost among them.

'I don't feel I belong here anymore.'

And with a look of concern, 'Has something happened?'

Perhaps she might understand my predicament? I wasn't after all suicidal.

'If you could pass our races' essential knowledge onto future generations, to make them greater, what would you choose?'

'Crikey Jason, that's a question not everyone, if anyone can answer.'

'Exactly. So why is no-one asking it?'

With her brief moment of thought I got this reply.

'Perhaps it is already being recorded in books, internet, monuments. It is whether we choose to acknowledge it. There, is that an answer?'

'Well, I was thinking the fundamentals starting in physics to chemistry, biology, psychology and philosophy. In that order. If we knew this as instinct and added to it, passing it on, then would this be our Genius Legacy?'

Was this too much for her to consider I ask?

'I think I better get you home.'

Good, I hoped I haven't alienated my only friend, I told myself.

Who was Mad Mike Hughes is a question I would hope you ask! We are inspired by many. Their character, their acts, their beliefs and their accomplishments left upon this world. Well, in the days before TV chefs and reality bores being the contemporary court room jesters were considered as influential, some led by example and became heroes to our future endeavours. Being like the Dare-Devil Evil Knievel, Mike Hughes was a thrill seeking Hollywood stunt man. He was famed for the longest Limo jump however what caught my attention was when he build a super heated steam powered rocket and launched himself 2 thousand feet into the air. Some claimed he was a Flat-Earthiest but most know he used their finance to both achieve his goals whilst highlighting their ridiculousness. He championed the 'Underdog' and inspired the masses that One can make a difference. The layman could be king! Like Spartacus, the slaves can be freed! The plebs can be enlightened, they can make a difference. Articles featuring

Mike's explosive exploits became an integral influence for my mission 'PROJECT EXODUS.' Initially this is a research file for neither the pointless or the faint hearted. When deeply engrossed with my future greatness it seemed society always attempted to break my line of thought, holding me back, denying my destiny. 'Jason! Your tea is on the table!' Despite being hollowed at from the depths below the stairs Mum couldn't distract me. Thanks to Mr Hughes, I had discovered a way! I wonder if Howard was related in any form? Both shared the same drive.

Slowly pushing peas around my plate wasn't a suggestion of being either full up or a distaste for them only envisaging the relationship between them. Either as people or atoms. Was there too much of a difference? If you put a large number in a confined space they eventually react the same. Becoming energized under the pressure to expand.

'You are very quiet these days son. Is everything OK at school?' My Dad asked waking me from my thoughts.

'Jason. Your father has asked you a question.' Mum wasn't so subtle.

'Can I have a rocket for my birthday?' I believe Mike was communicating with me through the power of suggestion with the peas.

'Your birthday isn't for a couple of months. What do you want a rocket for?'

I was in two minds whether Dad and Mum should be honoured or even understand where my destiny was leading.

'You still haven't told us where you've been today after school. Your father and I do worry Jason.'

'Sorry but I can't wait a couple of months. It's important and time is limited. Lets say a science experiment. Please?'

'Wouldn't you prefer a new bike?' Who was my Dad trying to fool!

'Don't they teach you those things in school? Science?' Mum asked.

I wished I had finance. I wouldn't have to negotiate and Project Exodus could happen a lot quicker. It seemed like the barriers were growing and all were trying to claw at me, delaying or holding me back.

'School is beneath me.' Is all I could reply with as being far from advising them the true extent of the beginnings from this initial experiment.

'Well Jason, judging from your recent school report it isn't. Your marks have gone down. 'Lacking in attention' your teachers have said.'

All I could do was advise thus:

'Education is what remains after one has forgotten what one has learned in school.' Albert Einstein. 'Now can I have a rocket?' So what do you think resulted from my mighty words of wisdom?

Yes, some few weeks later it had arrived! And my Dad and I were setting it up for launch in our local park. Conditions were perfect. A mostly clear bright sunny day, no wind, very few people which meant our privacy except for small group of kids playing football. As I made final checks monitoring the wind and making consequent notes on my clipboard, Dad unravelled the ignition wire to a safe distance.

'What ya doing?!' I heard over my shoulder.

Oh no it was the plebs playing football. I wasn't bothering their pointless games so what gives them the right to corrupt my investigations?

'A little science experiment with my son. So stand back it could be dangerous.' Dad advised.

As they approached I realised I recognised them.

'Isn't that kid from St Peters?'

'The Open Goalie!' They hollowed.

I asked myself, would these be the ones left behind? For what purpose do they serve our species?

'Are we good to go Dad?'

Their presence became muffled in the background as did my interest in such unenlightened cannon fodder.

'Planning a trip to the moon Jas!'

I ignored these cretins whilst Dad simply smiled as a kind man would do. With my back turned to them I took the control from Dad's hand and said aloft.

'5, 4, 3, 2, 1 Firing!'

The rocket burst into life and shot up into the air like something from the movies. Well in my mind anyway. Were the rabble inspired or impressed? I would like to think so. As its parachute deployed we gathered our belongings to collect it.

'Dad, how high do you think it reached?'

'I don't know. 200 metres?'

'Could we survive in space?'

'Not easily son. We are simply not built for it.'

Although I already knew the answers there is always the hope of unconsidered knowledge that came from being older with more experience in the world.

'Then how can we escape when the world comes to an end?'

How else would you expect a wise man to reply?

'Hopefully we might have figured it out before then.'

Hmm...

It was a clear morning and the moon was still visible in the sky as I sat staring out the class room window during a biology class. With the bell ringing for break and the other students eager to leave Mr Moreau's disenchanted voice echoed within the walls.

'I don't know why I bother wasting my breath on you lot. Have you been paying attention at all to my lesson? Jason?'

Turning from the window to see this man who at some point must have been wide eyed and full of wantem interest in his chosen field perhaps I could once more light his flame?

'Sir, what would humans need to do to survive a journey to the next habitable planet?'

'Jason, have you been listening to anything about today's lessons?'

'About yeast Sir?'

'So you're not totally away with the clouds.'

'Well Sir, could we survive?' And with baiting breath came the pathos.

'For someone who never pays attention, you certainly ask questions above the rest of the wantem horde. The answer is no. Space is too large and we are too frail and too short lived to cover any distance.'

'Is there anything that could?'

'You could look into micro-organisms. Tardigrades, bacteria and of course, yeast! Anything that survives or thrives inside or outside the International Space Station. Is this a school project?'

I couldn't tell him about 'Project Exodus.' It's too integral and still top secret at its early stage of development.

'No Sir, perhaps a calling? Thanks Mr Moreau.' And with this I made a hasty exit to become lost among the others before any suspicion could be mustered.

I believe most metaphors are derived from experience. In acting out one's beliefs furthers the experiment especially for the cause of trial and error. So I found myself crossing a stream via the stepping stones back and forth to hopefully attain clarity. And like a fateful circumstance my path and Mary's aligned.

'What are you doing?' She inquisitively asked.

'If it is not possible to physically reach our destination then we can take smaller steps before leap-frogging onto the next. Understand?'

Perhaps I was throwing her in the deep end rather than preparing her with the conversational spring board.

'I don't think anyone understands you. Do you?'

Maybe she had a point? Clarity of meaning is required so I tried another angle.

'Why is your Dad a vicar?'

'Because he believes in hope and to inspire hope in others'

'And why are you an aestheticist?' She looked shocked.

'I'm not! Who told you? What makes you think,'

And with the physical gestures between the stepping stones, 'It takes faith to leap. Hope to see the other side and with ever step we evolve to reach the next.'

My words of wisdom bit back with the final leap as I slipped into the water and Mary inevitably laughed!

'Perhaps your lacking in hope!' I too could only laugh with this eventuality.

'Perhaps Darwin's natural selection!' I speedily replied.

Taking my hand she pulled me back onto the embankment.

'And perhaps we better get you home.' Her hands felt warm and reassuring.

'Did you ever consider having my child?'

I remember she responded with a warm smile.

'Ask me again when you are no longer one!'

Do you ever get the feeling that your crimes eventually catch up with you when it seems luck has been less forth coming? I was in my bedroom researching as usual for 'Project Exodus' when I heard a loud knock at the front door. I deemed such disturbances as a crime in themselves. Mum answered it as I crept onto the landing. 'John!'

Dad was in the lounge fixing selves.

'What is it love?' '

'You better come here!'

And there in our hallway stood a policeman with Mum looking distressed.

'What has the little sh, sugar done?' Mum trying to be restrained.

'Jason has been caught on CCTV stealing books from the Public Library' he advised.

'What! I haven't brought up a criminal.'

Dad entered the scene as the calming voice of reason.

'What's going on?'

'Your son in a thief!' She dramatically replied.

'I'm sure there is a perfectly rational explanation to all this.'

Mum seemed to be getting more erratic of late, perhaps she's going through the change I thought.

'What ever are the neighbours going to think?!'

The Officer advised no charges were being pressed however I would receive a caution and I had to return the removed property.

'But why Jason? I don't understand?'

The real question is would Mum understand?

'Pioneers need to take risks to discover and expand their boundaries.'

'Don't give me any of that talk of yours. Your boundaries will be your bedroom until further notice!'

And with that I was persecuted and sent to my exile. Funny enough, that suited me fine! As I headed up stairs I heard Dad.

'Will he have a criminal record?'

'John, we'll have to move. There's no way I can hold my head up in decent society. It's all your fault. You are too soft with him. I blame you. I blame that harlot, the Vicar's daughter!'

Out of a strange curiosity away from my studies, I left my bedroom door ajar to listen in.

'I knew it would lead to this.'

'It's only a few books. No real harm done Martha.'

'It's just the beginning. What happens when he's out of control later on? What happens when he finds out?'

'Martha, He's old enough. He'll understand.'

'All I tried to do was offer a better chance for him.'

'I should of seen this coming. I mean, what do you think was going to happen when after-all he came from that thing?!'

'He's only a growing boy Martha. We all make mistakes.'

'It's all about the breeding and you knew we couldn't have one of our own at that time. But I never expected this.'

'He's a very special boy and just a bit different from the others. Gifted.'

'Gifted? He's manipulative. Like a devil. He's not the boy in the basket.'

'Martha, I think your blowing this out of proportion. Why don't you go and have rest. I'll make the tea.'

'This is now but what about what happens next and after next?'

I shouldn't have been eavesdropping as ominous questions stifle my mental becoming.

'Perhaps we should tell him?'

And with that I closed my bedroom door.

To keep Mum happy and all else, the following day I returned the books. The Librarian was a kind lady who didn't understand the purpose of this theft let alone the fact I had read them all. I kindly advised there is deeper meaning to the act then there was in the content. Of course I was slightly lying, however who was she to know? On my return home I decided to take the short cut across the stream where the stepping stones reside. I heard a moaning coming from the long grass above the embankment. Could it be an animal in distress? No! it was what Shakespeare described as 'The Beast with two backs.' To my shock and dismay it was Mary lying on her back with some delinquent giving it to her! All I could do to stop him was hurl lumps of mud.

'Get off her scum bag! Get off her!' I shouted.

'Jason? Stop it! Stop it Jason. It's not what you think!'

'Getting soiled by this scum!' Get off her!'

'What the fXXk! Who's this kid?!' Delinquent Dale hollowed whilst attempting to pull his trousers up and avoid the incoming mud bombs.

'He's just a boy from the church.'

It was at this point a well aimed mud bomb struck Dale directly in this acne ridden face!

'FXXk off!!' he screamed.

And then something quite odd erupted from my mouth. 'She won't give you a baby! She's mine!'

Mary was somewhat shocked and Dale had recovered to his feet and began pursuit. 'Get back here you little shit! You fXXcking little pervert!!' I recall him saying or words to that effect. However being less practised than I crossing the stepping stones, Dale slipped in and I escaped hearing Mary calling after me.

Arguments had become an increasingly common situation in our house. Holding a pillow over my ears I sat staring at the books which I didn't return to the library. My special trophies I would call them. And I had a word with myself.

'There are too many distractions. A great mind needs time to think. To enter into one's exile to gain clarity and compose.

So I will simply stop talking. I will become withdrawn like Geoffrey Archer and Hitler using this time as if incarcerated.'

However Meinkampt is not what I will be looking to formulate.

That night I fell asleep with the song from The Doors whirling around my head, 'Riders on the Storm.' I dreamt of a baron lifeless desert and I silhouetted disappearing into the sunset. I believe I am to join the ranks of Buddha, Moses and Jim Morrison, to exponentially extend my knowledge and then allow the universe to dictate my consequent actions. For I am, The Chosen One!

Do nightmares truly exist or is it our subconscious trying to tell us something? The Mayans thought so. The 3 Neutron Stars were calling me once more however they faded into two, rapidly accelerating towards me, striking through glass to the abrupt screams of my parents. I awoke to the face of a large smiling Jamaican nurse and a doctor flashing a torch into my eyes. Was I dead? No just unresponsive.

'And how do you feel today Jason?' The Nurse asked with her kind and gentle voice in a somewhat predictive manner. At one point I believed I knew what people were about to say before they said it. Like I was reading their lines from a play. I didn't know whether I was part of the audience or one of the players. I used to ask questions where I already knew their response only to observe their characteristics. Did Laurence Olivier suffer the same?

'Jason? I know you are in there. What are you thinking? What do you see?'

I looked at my hands that seemed somewhat aged from the last time I considered such matters. I tried to respond to her.

'I only see what I need to be.' However no words emitted from my mouth.

She turned to who I can only assume was the doctor.

'Where do you think he is?'

'Far away, sadly. But I'm positive he will return. Just a matter of time.'

I closed my eyes.

I opened the bedroom curtains to see Dad digging a hole in the back garden. Unusual behaviour for him so I had to investigate even though I was still sporting my Doctor Strange pyjamas.

'What are you doing Dad?'

'Morning Jason. I'm doing a little experiment. Can you pass me that stainless steel cylinder?'

Had my influence rubbed off on him or was I his student all along?

'What's all this stuff?'

'Well son. It's a time machine. But not like the such of H.G Wells ideologies.'

'I doesn't look like one.'

'We place today's newspaper with a picture of ourselves and a sample of our hair for DNA. And lastly a little something I have put together on this flash drive. We bury it deep into the ground, hidden for future generations to discover it. And when the time might be right the Earth will push it to the surface . Our future generations will know who we were and what our world was like. We would have travelled into the future beyond our mortal existences.'

We sealed the container and planted it. It felt great that Dad was sharing this experiment with me as we covered it over with soil and reassuringly patted the earth on top of the time capsule.

'There we go son. You, your mum and I are now closer to being immortal!' He said with a cheeky smile.

'What does that mean?' being over analytical.

'Our memory may not be forgotten.'

One memory I wished I had forgotten but forever tormented me was the day I found out. I confronted them during a car journey where there was nowhere to avoid the truth.

'Don't lie! I heard you! You're not my mum!' I screamed.

'Shut up Jason you don't know.' Said Mum.

'Know what? I'm adopted. I want my real Mum!'

'She didn't want you. She was a low life crack whore!'

'You don't want me either now your finally up the duff!'

'Jason!' Dad shouted.

'You're not my flesh and blood. You're not my past. I'm not your future!'

And that is when it happened. Stereotypically, fate stepped in with a truck broadsiding us. Mum was killed instantly and Dad was thrown from the car to later die from his injuries I was told. I was in a coma for some time before being transferred to a mental health hospital.

Fate is a cruel dictator. Am I now truly alone?

'Hi Jason. How are you feeling? I've brought you some books from your list. I also found your Dad's journal.'

Did I really need any further excuses to be further withdrawn into the world of science and philosophy? My room gave the impression of an earth-quake in a library. However I tried to smile as she stood before me silhouetted against the window. The shards of sunlight creating her aurora. She was like a vision beaconing me back to the life. My saviour. My Mary Magdalene. The Nurse disrupted my admiration of my saving angel.

Mary asked, 'Has he talked?'

'Not a breath. Lost in his own world. Aren't you Jason. A little genius without a voice.'

I might be older however I wasn't ready for any scrap heap. Only 16 but feeling far removed from childhood.

'Perhaps a caterpillar waiting to burst out of his cocoon. Is the coffee machine still broken?'

'Fixed this morning.'

'Would you like one?'

'No thank you lovely.'

Mary left me with her.

'Whatever is going on in there Jason? It's a beautiful day and you are caging yourself away from this world. All these books have become your bars. It's time to start living again. Life is too short.'

The Nurse left but her mighty words of wisdom was indicative of Einstein's!

'the man who regards his own life and that of his fellow-creatures as meaningless is not merely unfortunate but almost disqualified from life.'

The time of theory was at an end! I picked up my Dad's journal entitled 'Ingenio Legatum' (Genius Legacy) and made my hasty exit.

With research reaching completion it was time for the practical so with my parent's life assurance payout I had to find a property that would both serve as a domicile as well as a laboratory come workshop. I understand that Victor Frankenstein's crib was unavailable however I discovered a property bordering on the town's outskirts where the closest neighbour was a farm a mile down the road. This seemed perfect. A small dwelling with garden, garage and large shed. I only required the basics. A bed, kitchen and bathroom. But the rest to be utilised for experiments and engineering.

No noise, no adjoining neighbours, cheap rent and low light pollution for my telescope. This was the perfect place.

Fate was beginning to favour me.

The landlord was the farmer from down the road. He seemed careless to what occurred here just as long as the rent was paid on time and he wouldn't be bothered on a regular basis. Or at all!

'You can have it as long as you like. When it comes to leaving, place needs to be in the same condition as when moved in. OK?'

I agreed, signed the lease and with his exit began my mission. The shed roof would have to be opened to work as an observation platform for my telescope as well as a broadcast area for a radio and laser transmitters. The garage would be my engineering department and the large spare room to be the laboratory.

Sadly a man is not an octopus! So with only one pair of hands this might take some time. I would like help or an assistant but how could I trust them? And by the time I explained the task ahead I could of completed it myself. Besides, it isn't a job so payment would be irrelevant. It's a passion, it's an obsession, it's a necessity to ensure our survival and how can any assistant feel the same as I? Afterall, they are not 'The chosen one!'

It took many months of labour before finally being able to begin my experiments. I did concern myself with the prospect of becoming a character like Nikola Tesla. All efforts on work to the expense of health. I didn't want to ostracize myself from society as my purpose was to save them. Also I didn't want to become so utterly consumed by my work that my brain would finally fail me and I would find solace in the eyes of a pigeon! I didn't really want to fall in love with anything or anyone however life cannot continue to exist unaided.

As a consequence I looked into the mirror to ask myself where all these demanding tasks have left me?

3.
The Virile Necessity

If we do not breed the cell does not evolve. We do not survive. Simple.

I find myself standing upon a bridge overlooking a river envisaging tadpoles escaping their egg sacks. I study the sticks and leaves being carried along the surface bouncing off rocks upon their journey. And I consider this. From energy to atoms, particles to cells to amoeba to fish to reptiles to mammals, we have crawled out of the water. Egyptian and Mayan cultures suggest we could have derived from an outer alien influence. Nature, nurture, regardless. One thing is certain. We adapt and evolve. That is our true strength.

I drop a stone into the slow running river to observe the expanding rings. And let me tell you this: The universe is expanding and we will be stranded on this sinking island if we don't reach out beyond. Despite the impossible odds of reaching an interstellar shore, I will build a raft. If Robinson Crusoe survived with a vision of hope and a reluctance to stagnate then so must we.

As I crossed the bridge I saw a frog leaping into the water. Further down the embankment is where the stepping stones reside. And this is where I must cross indeed. I! Yes I will engineer our greatest knowledge into a biological housing that can be transported to new environments where it can flourish and once again leap onto the next. To metaphorically, consistently crawl out of the water. My mortal coil is my only constraint. All distractions and non-essentials will be discarded. My Occam's Razor.

I stare into the waters surface to reveal a countenance no longer suffering the innocence of adolescence but a frail disturbed face of a man bearing everything to gain with the past willing to do so. I stub out my cigarette and believe donning a dressing gown out in public might not be the statement I need to make anymore.

It is imperative my time is vigorously protected and optimally utilised whilst defending against the threat from risk and aiding my health. This is what I said to myself whilst avoiding contact with the general public walking through the bustling high street. I might of received the odd look as I was sporting a facemask and surgical gloves but was this any different to the odd rules all had to comply with during Covid?

'You fXXking idiot!! Are you blind?!!' Is what I heard from a bus driver as I had inadvertently stepped into his path whilst trying to avoid the a coughing school girl. With a mind so occupied it was easy to become less focused on the obvious. After-all even Einstein used to forget to put his socks on!

And where was I mentally that day? Walking through a field of long grass during a warm summer's evening. With the seeds rising into the air upon the gentle breeze as my hands combed through them. Very idealistic to gather one's thoughts.

Reality was somewhat different as I viewed myself in the bathroom mirror. In the world of epigenetics where external factors influence our DNA I have come to the conclusion that all these years in exile have resulted in an unhealthy, fat, egotistical, drunken, chain-smoking slob! Perhaps Nietzsche was right. I need to become the Ubermensch and lead by example. And what has happened to the young man who left the hospital as our species saviour? Well he got a little distracted along the way lets say. However with a new dawn rises the new man!

Looking like a dilapidated tramp I threw open the lounge curtains to allow light to break into my lab. Cracking open a window to permit air in whilst the stench out. It was time to clear the decks and fill the black bin liners. All signs of degradation had to go. The overflowing ashtrays, the half eaten pizzas, the Indian takeaways, the bottles of wine and whisky. The now unrequired stacks of research articles all had to go. The first action we do as a newborn is to breathe. So why have I been denying this simple pleasure? So out with the cigarettes! I cast them into the bin! And with clearance comes clarity.

With a cleared house next is a cleared me. I'm sure this will work as I drink a bottle of laxative and wait with a baited arse for nature to call before embarking on the dash to the toilet. Equally I will give myself a colonic irrigation utilising my garden hose pipe, inserting it where the sun refuses to shine.

'Out with the evil!' I screamed!!

'And now we may begin!'

And with a complete shower, shave and haircut I do believe I could pass for a civilised member of society.

I am sporting the finest headband and shell suit jogging through the park whilst reminiscing of the days I would be smoking, drinking, and waking in a puddle of vomit. And I tell myself that was yesterday's man. However as I collapse on a park bench sweating profusely. I am far off the gains gathered by the health-o-holics that I bear witness to. I can feel their laughter upon me. Maybe they started at my level? But they seemed twisted with self-righteousness. My animosity or jealousness could not take this further. I felt the need to defend my honour.

'Why attempt to extend your existences if you have no purpose!' I expelled.

I could only improve with the regularity of practice and the will to perform such endeavours.

Having tidied the kitchen, clearing the old, the mouldy and the processed I had a little think to myself whilst chomping on a carrot. I believe in chemistry. I believe in biology. I believe in plight of the North American Indians. I don't know if consuming tiger balls make you more virile but essentially you are what you eat! Metal will decay if consumed by salt. Pure water and nutrients will fuel cell strength. This is organic. So I took a bite of raw garlic. It might of tasted disgusting however it was feasible and I proved to be no vampire!

I imagined myself stood upon the summit of a mountain, arms outstretched as the image of Christ the Redeemer. And shouting aloft

'This is the fable of the king who lived to excess but relinquished all in search for the magic mirror of youth and vitality. There was no magic mirror only the efforts searching for it madeth the man!'

I looked into the bathroom mirror to better understand the fable as I was sporting a healthier being.

My laboratory was cladded in white-boards featuring the mathematics from Escape Velocities to Cell Reproduction and the Drake's Equation. My books were neatly arranged on shelves according to their purpose. And I had an array of biospheres at various stages of their development. At this point I would cook many of my evening meals here as if an experiment. Meat balls, ousters marinaded in Guinness fried over a Bunsen burner.

Life is too short and should the constraints of time prevent my quest from being forfilled then my future generations will have no option but to become successful. The only problem is how would one breed when I am not what the female seeks? And like an exploding star I realised I have to change. As in nature, it is the female that picks the male. My feathers must be brighter than my peacock competition! For I can parade higher with grandeur

My hunt began sat in a bar where the humans gathered to let their guard down whilst intoxifying theirselves. 'Pay to be poisoned' should be the business' motto. I sit quietly and unassuming amongst the heathen hordes studying the competition's profiles on my mobile. According to my studies, today's male presents themselves as sensitive but with an edge of danger. Steroid induced muscles sporting beards and blouses. Perhaps gay lumberjacks? If our generation is confused about who they are then how can they be focused on the future? Maybe I have got this wrong? A female seeks a partner who is a warrior when facing others whilst being a slave to their needs? Maybe the males know this and are adhering to the female's nature for procreation? I sit here and observe the interactions between a group of males all jousting for the best position around the watering hole. Like pack animals lets presume?

Well not having a pack of my own I'm trying an alternative. I find myself in disguise sat on a bench in the park during a lunch time where the herd gather. I ask myself would the females spot my fake beard and muscles? Would they pay attention to my lady's blouse? And on a sensory element would they succumb to the deer musk? I receive no attention. Perhaps I have become invisible. Perhaps this approach has proved unsuccessful which guides me to gaze up to the sun. Entropy, where all atoms are reduced to their natural state of chaos. I am 30. The average male lives to 85. That's 55 years I have to complete my mission should nothing break my path. The gene needs to survive. But there is little time to breed and parent. Being bait it is time to cast out my hook and line as 2 female joggers pass. I hoped my best rehearsed smile isn't perceived as anything but great intentions. On passing they look away as if I was some kind of dangerous freak. It's all a matter of trial and error I tell myself. So I need to adapt.

Later that evening I put aside my other engineering efforts and experiments in favour of further research. Subjects being Rudolf Valentino, Barry White and Vic Reeves. Although looks aren't always everything but charm with the element of the unexplainable something could be the key. Conclusions suggest courtship is a dance. The initial weaving of souls. To capture a bird of paradise, appearance is the initial bait with a display of sexual prowess followed by emotional engagement, passion in direction, also humour? With wealth perhaps as the final net? Unlike the Milk Tray Man I couldn't simply like a horse whisperer or like a mystic becoming her curiosity, seduce a lady by breaking into her house leaving her chocolates before diving off a waterfall making a hasty exit.

With the aid of YouTube teaching videos I grab a pillow and practice the courtship dances of the foxtrot, waltz, salsa and tango accidentally knocking into the odd bit of furniture along the way. I say to myself what lady could refuse to submit after witnessing my flamenco!

'You alone can make my song take flight. Help me make the music of the night.'

Is this natural or am I her Phantom? All seems pre-orchestrated with a strategy when passion is left out of the equation. Does this make one a predator? Oh well, needs dictate I assure myself. And lastly, with a touch of modernism, Bony M, 'Rasputin' to liven it up somewhat. What bird of paradise could flutter away once caught in my web of courtship?

'Well, you can tell by the way I use my walk, I'm a woman's man: no time to talk.

The music loud and the women warm, I've been kicked around since I was born.'

With the Bee Gees tune singing loud in my head I ventured to the local night club dressed as John Travolta. How apt was this to 'Project Exodus', Stayin' Alive I proudly told myself. It simply made sense and was indeed one of fate's cogs.

Venturing inside the venue I received a dramatic shock as all I rehearsed could have been a grave mistake. Unknowing to I, it was a Drum & Bass club and I stood out like a candyfloss machine at robot wars! Nevertheless, I was here and despite the looks mostly resulting in laughter, I hit the dance floor like an asteroid striking the Earth. Maybe a tad out of sync I admit but I received respect from the Disc Jockey and many of the club's visitors took pictures with their mobile phones. My theories must have become a reality when I was joined by a group of ladies all of which were lightly attired lets say. As they gathered closer and became increasingly flirtatious, I thought it's time to make my move. Although I couldn't quite hear her name, I believe it was Trinity, I decided to employ my sure thing move on this young lady. I applied pelvic thrusts to secure her as mine. She seemed very agreeable to this suggestion and I believe our moves became something oddly reminiscent to the Lambada, The Forbidden Dance! However, little to my knowledge at the time, her boyfriend, Tarquin felt otherwise. This vast beast of a man lifted me by the collar as if I was a rag doll before applying a fist to my face. Ouch! Severely not the end result to conclude my experiment. I thought to myself whilst lying there in a pool of blood and being ignored by the other dancers with consequently being dragged out by the bouncers, that perhaps an intimate approach is better required.

Inside my lab, I paced like a caged beast. I thought there must be a mathematical way of improving my odds. And there in front of me stood the answer as if my subconscious was guiding me. The Drake's Equation! The method of suggesting the probability of life other celestial planets. Quite simply, you take the number of stars in the sky, then the ones with planets within their habitual zone. And then those which are able to sustain life. Sounds straight forward. Apparently he produced this as a tad of a joke!

I openly admit, I am probably not the only person to consider its structure to determine an alternative.

So you take the number of women within your cited area. Subtract those outside of your breeding bracket and availability. Subtract those who you don't share a mutual interest and those who aren't willing to breed. Against the probability of meeting and engaging with them. This leaves the answer. I do believe the National Lottery might have better odds! Unless ofcourse you surround yourself within a richer target environment. The Singles Night!

And this is where I next found myself. In a wine bar trying to look normal amongst the desperate and needy. Was I anything different I ask myself as I sit alone in a corner? However it seemed strangely different to my previous efforts. A lady, although a little bit mature for my purposes approached. I thought to myself, do I look virile and wealthy? Perhaps I was being unnecessarily critical and should just let nature work her magic.

'Hi. My name is Katy. Would you like some company?'

I smiled and nodded beckoning her over. Even acting as a gentleman by pulling out a chair.

'Uh, sure. Be my guest.' I tried to hide any nervousness before becoming devoured.

'You don't seem to be like the others here?'

Unsure how to examine this, I remained reserved.

'How do I differ?'

'Well just look at them. Desperate, sweaty and over eager to please. Talking bollocks in the vain attempt to sound interesting and to gain our trust. It's so false. Are there any real men around?'

Was she feeling comfortable in my company? Did she think I was gay? Should I too be sweaty and desperate?

'Perhaps they feel time is escaping them and they fear for being left out?' I responded.

'So what's your secret?'

Was she a love spy? What could I tell her? I could only try. I hoped I wouldn't come across as a person outside of her interest.

'Darwin identified evolution and Dawkins saw it as a mutation of the gene, consistently developing to surpass its survival challenges. I need an heir however attaining one has never been so complex with demands being so pre-orchestrated.' She sat back for a moment in quiet contemplation.

'Would you like to get out of here?' She asked to my surprise. Was she going to 'give it to me?' But she is outside my target range.

'I don't think we share the same chemistry' was my stupid response. Although I might consider myself The Chosen One, a genius, on this occasion my brain worked less than that of an amoeba's.

'Oh, I see. Well good luck finding your utopia. 'Cause there's no fuckin' chance in here!'

And with that she left and I was once more was sat alone feeling like a confused lab rat. I didn't mean to offend only to be honest and scientific about the process.

As I sit here trawling through what seems to be as endless dating websites I contemplate how the world has changed. So many ladies' profiles all seem to be selling their souls. Was arranged marriages such a bad thing I think? Meeting by chance is proving too improbable and old fashion. A target rich environment remains my only option. Singles nights, speed-dating and internet courtship. All of which has become commercial. Cupid has become a profiteering pimp! A mercenary to our desires. Oh, the humanity of it! If it is propaganda to force belief then so be it! I too should advertise myself. I took a picture as if a proud leader and entered a description worthy of a Shakespearian sonnet.

I seek a woman who has focus and believes in a future. One who is compassionate, spiritual and adventurous. Let me be your gentleman. Let me be your scoundrel but let me become the reality to your hopes, desires and dreams. Together we can be as one, for I am your Valentino, your Casanova, your Romeo. And you dear lady, my Juliet, my princess, my queen, my Guinevere.

'I can't fail with this' I proudly told myself and posted it online. I'm sure a torrent of responses will soon be flooding in so I sat back and watched a documentary about the intricate dance of the male Australian Jumping Spider. Would I suffer a similar fate? The hunter becoming the hunted? If successful, waiting to be consumed. I also feel like a can of Baked Beans on an endless supermarket shelf. Perhaps discarded without being tasted? Swipe left, swipe right, being that disposable. Courting has never been so tailored initiated on appearance alone. I close my eyes and await the ping from a reply.

With the gentle ring of the shopkeepers doorbell she walks into the restaurant. Folding away her umbrella and managing her long soft locks of auburn hair this beautiful lady, Emily, greets me with a smile. She seems like a fallow deer taking a cautious sip from the river's edge.

'Hi Emily. I made an educated guess and got you a glass of Rosetta. I hope this is OK?'

'You're not what I was expecting.'

'Is that a good or bad thing?' I questioned with desired hope as she glances around observing the other couples enjoying their romantic meals. I passed Emily a menu.

'How is your appetite? Anything you desire?' I asked rasing my eyebrow as if Roger Moore.

'Actually, I'm sorry but you're not what I'm looking for. I don't wish to waste your time. And I've arranged to meet a friend.'

I felt as skewered as the carcasses upon the diners' plates. I had to recover this date.

'If you could give me just 2 minutes of your precious time, you might make a decision that will change your life and echo through eternity. I'll guarantee all those women sat with their other halves will be incredibly jealous when they see you walking out the door with me.'

How could she not be intrigued?

'You're very sure of yourself.' She replied.

'Would you like to know a little secret?' I leant forward to whisper into her ear.

'You are a beautiful ripe female and are destined to bear my heir. Like Moses, I will save mankind from extinction for I am The Chosen One.' I sat back. She seemed speechless before emptying the glass of Rosetta over my head, laughing as she left. A stunned silence broke across the restaurant, as the diners tried to remain resigned to my situation. All I could do was sit back, realise the comedy of my mistake with a sigh and a giggle. The waitress handed me a towel.

'Is there anything else I can get you?' She asked with an awkwardly smile.

'Perhaps Darwin was mistaken!' I replied.

Leaving the restaurant heading towards the taxi rank I felt it only right to place a tenner into the deer stalking hat of a sleeping homeless lady. Maybe as an apology to the gender I had just inadvertently insulted.

Finding a mate was proving an unimaginable expense on my time when considering all the other demands expected by 'Project Exodus.' I felt my options were running out and maybe as a further insult to my integrity I returned to the singles bar. I sat down and observed a rather fat bold man in the company of a younger lady sporting a revealing dress with heavy make-up. She appeared to be accommodating to his advances. Was he being baited? After my previous efforts I do believe I was becoming un-necessarily cynical. Without meaning to be dehumanising, the female's biological needs demand the fittest gene from their suitor, matching the facilitator for its successful development. In other words, attraction, health, wealthy and obedience, while engaging her hopes and dreams. To woe a lady one needs to act as a predator when in reality it is the female who chooses the male. The keys to the palace gates are not held by us knights! This was my concluding hypothesis as once again I was inside the lair of the needy, lonely and desperate. One should tread carefully I told myself.

I spotted a rather nice looking lady on her mobile phone sat across the room from me. The time was now or never. Every gentleman's nightmare was the rejection of a lady. So being brave I approached her.

'Hi, my name is Jason. May I join you?'

'Anna. I'm not staying long but please do.'

'What brings you here? You don't seem like the type who is short of attention.' I said attempting to appeal to her sense of grandeur.

'Well, I would like to say I'm having an experiment with fate.'

'I know the feeling.' Were such parallels justified? Fate? She was speaking my language.

'I suppose the typical question of conversation starters would be what do you do?'

Not an easy one to answer so I thought I'd present a simplistic approach.

'I'm a rocket scientist. And you?'

'I work in mental health.'

'Is there a fine line between madness and invention?' I asked in jest to avoid being her test subject whilst paying homage to Barnes Wallis.

'Possibly. How do you see yourself? A genius? A maverick? A pioneer?'

'Far from it. Perhaps lucky enough to be enlightened. I'm working on a very special and unique project.'

'Well I have a couple of minutes before my taxi arrives. I'm all ears. Tell me more.' Heavens above I thought. Here was a attractive lady who was actually interested in mental stimulation with I. Was she the one?

'A couple of minutes isn't long enough. Can I call you? We could meet up? You could take my number. Have my card.'

With a glance at the time and a smile she gathered her coat.

'Thanks. Perhaps lets leave it to fate.'

What was this to mean? A further rejection or containing something more? Perhaps an understanding of cosmic alignment? I would wait with baited breath.

And then there is the daunting speed dating. Where 4 minute interrogations determine how pathetic one another is! Perhaps I'm being over sceptical as the bell rings and we all change chairs like a merry-go-round or the Maypole Dance. In my head I hear Matthias Claudius' 'We plough the fields and scatter...' in the style of café bar jazz. There before me was a lady of neat appearance. Very well to do.

'Hi, my name is Judy. How are you?'

This breaks the protocol I was expecting. The typical questions being: Who are you? What do you do and how much do you earn? My scepticism knows no bounds but should I really be like this? After-all I'm not attending as an experiment. I need a host for my endeavours. They are human too and must equally possess more than I imagine them to be.

'Hi Judy, I'm Leonardo. May I ask, what's the most impressive thing you've done and you want to do?' I asked with a gentle smile.

'Well, let me see. I've love travelling and I've been to over 100 countries. The mountains in Tibet were to die for for! Where have you been?'

She leaned forward with baited interest and I couldn't tell her nowhere! So I thought be yourself and speak from the heart.

'I'm hoping to travel to the stars.'

'Oh, I see...?'

Sitting back I could see she thought I wasn't her type. Perhaps Judy saw me as a hapless fool, a dreamer or a mad delusional loser? And as an awkward silence descended, Judy was saved by the bell and I moved on.

I had to refocus my approach. The following woman had darker hair and looked less agreeable. Her name tag stated 'Mandy.'

'Why hello my little bird of paradise.' I said in jest.

'Hi, just to save time. What do you do? Where are you from and how much do you earn?'

I hardly believe this is the way to get to know one another. Although direct she came across a tad rude or simply impatient so I constructed a reply worthy of her disposition!

'Hi. I'm Nikola. I'm a visionary from Ascension Island. And I earn knowledge and direction. Yourself?'

'But your name tag says Leonardo? Are you a weirdo?'

'Throughout history visionaries have been perceived as outcasts.'

'That doesn't sound like much fun to me.'

'Perhaps that's because I'm not on your horizon.'

I don't think I would score highly on her contact card after this whole performance ended. And there rang the bell.

The next woman appeared a little rough round the edges however she seemed to sport very kind hazel eyes. Funny enough that was her name. I hoped for better luck.

'Are you my Casanova?'

She took a nervous sip of red wine. Her hands were shaking. Poor lamb I thought. And I the wolf?

'Prey on a vulnerable lady? Be attentive, extricate her from her difficulty, bestow small gifts, use alluring words, make hay, get bored and escape?'

'That's not what I meant.'

Although I was only trying to consul her as to that which I was not, I could see my methods were spiralling out of true intent becoming misconceived.

'Do you believe us men are predators?' I tried to say reassuringly.

'I'm just here for a bit of fun.'

''Then victims?' Where were my verbal brakes I mentally hailed myself!

'I just thought there would be some nice men here.' She was becoming increasingly anxious whilst looking for an out. Did my predecessor upset her or was it me?

'Sorry I didn't mean to upset you.' I leant forward attempting to hold her hand but she hastily withdrew hers.

'You have no idea of how to treat a lady!'

And with that I retreated. Oops! She could have been the one if not for being over emotional. Or was it I whose intent was misconceived? Poorly communicated? My orchestra of intention was performing a overture rather than a ballad.

Theresa looked like a better candidate. She appeared more mature than the others with a wilder look maybe gathered from experience.

'And what would be your perfect date?' She asked in a fashion of promiscuity.

'One where all pretences are forsaken. Where you don't have to dress up and be fake to impress. Where we can examine each others' true beings.'

'I like the sound of that. Tell me more!'

'How about you tell me young lady.' I too could play flirtatious.

'Hmm. What about us as tramps on a date to a park? Our entertainment being people watching as if in a theatrical play? Maybe even naked? Like in the short film, Mindgames & Playgrounds.'

'Yes, Observing the species in their natural surrounds.'

'What would that say about us? Merely spectators?'

'Hopefully more. Is that what is occurring here?' I asked rhetorically.

She replied with a smile. Was I naked I her eyes? Although I felt very vulnerable she intrigued me and I hoped she would score me for a future date.

The bell rang.

Reaching the conclusion of the evening I had two dates left. I couldn't see the next lady's name tag as she was hunched over her mobile phone. A bit rude I thought. She had a short red leather skirt, fishnet tights reaching into her thigh long boots. Her mammaries looked like they could feed the five thousand I thought to myself! As I sat she leaned back with an almighty yawn that only a dentist would appreciate for access.

'I've sat here listening to every type of desperate rodent trying to weasel their way into my knickers. So why should I listen to you?'

Gob-smacked I replied, 'If it were the 1950's, they'd say you've got spunk!'

And finally a well built, heavily made up woman of a rather masculine physique ended my last date with,

'Are you the male or female of the species?' It asked!!

And with that I left. I congratulated myself that despite these failures I was at least brave enough to attend and learn from my experiences. After-all most experiments are a case of trial and error.

It was a cold night and my breath gathered like exhaled clouds as I waited at the taxi rank. At least I was heading home to the warmth that the indoors could offer unlike the poor homeless soul who sat behind me encased in blankets with only a Deer Stalker hat to gather income to stove off the inevitable. I found myself blanking out the city's barrage of distractions and looking up above beyond the buildings. If the cosmos is trying to give me a sign then perhaps it's one without light. It seemed as if my attempts to attain a mother for an heir was proving unsuccessful. Perhaps fate is my cruel mistress? And with that thought in mind I felt a vibration in my trouser pocket. My mobile phone.

'Hello?'

'Hi. We met last week. It's Anna. Would you like to meet?'

'Uh, sure? What ever happened to fate?'

'Lets say, this is fate. I was only just thinking of you.'

'When and where shall we meet then Anna?'

'I'll text you OK?'

Curious I thought to myself. I recall her being a mental health nurse. I hope I am not her test subject. Checking the notes in my pocket as the taxi arrived I believe it was only right to aid the poor homeless soul behind me. I could spare a tenner so that is what I placed into the hat.

'Thank you.' The homeless person lifted her head and stared what seemed to be through me. 'Jason?'

There was something familiar here. I recognised that sweet, sweet voice.

'Mary?'

4.

TO BE INFLUENCED

I do not wish to state the obvious only to shed light upon the forgotten or ignored reality. So I found a theatrical way to reach the people.

Dressed in the robes like a biblical messiah, I find myself upon a soap box in Speakers Corner standing before a mobile phone touting crowd. I only hope they share this performance to the world as I paraphrase another's words of wisdom.

'To every person upon this Earth, Death cometh soon or late. And I ask myself, how can a man die better than facing fearful odds for the ashes of his fathers, and the temples of his Gods. We are all heretics standing on the bridge. Our enemy is time. Everything you know is irrelevant unless we evolve and reach beyond. Don't let life hold you back. Don't let others push us into extinction. Evolution is within our grasp if we confront the enemies of our beings.'

'Who the fXXk is that then?!' Was a voice I heard from the herd.

'Open your eyes and tell me who threatens your survival and your generation's that succeed you.'

'Illegal immigrants!'

'No my child' I said calmly.

'Gangs!? Terrorists?! '

'No.' I couldn't say not everyone has an ideology that isn't always in sync with ours.

'The Government!'

'No. If a Government is as corrupt as the people, what choice do they give themselves?'

'Who then?' A female in a large brimmed summers hat called.

'If life is out of balance and the Earth can no longer facilitate our growing numbers then a reduction is our only option. Natural de-selection to those who depose our generation's survival.'

'Didn't Hitler have the same idea?!' I heard from a rather disgruntled elderly gent.

I was loosing their attention as their mobile cameras were lessening to capture my message and they began to disperse.

'Hitler sought control. Hitler sought genocide. Hitler didn't see an Exodus from this madness!!'

Sadly I was now preaching to the Heavens as they had all but gone.

Should I really be relying on the herd's nature to broadcast my message when I can do such myself? So I sat in my laboratory, creating a blog!

'History demands a record of reasoning behind the efforts that made our turning point. Here is mine for the inspiration of our future generations and leadership whilst acting as a caution to error.'

'Jason. I've made you some coffee.' I heard from the lounge.

'Thanks, I'll be with you in a minute.'

I wasn't use to such delightful interruptions however she was my saving angel and I could always return to my blog.

'Thank you for letting me stay.' Mary looked at home sipping her coffee and wrapped up in a warm blanket on my couch.

'What are you doing on the streets? Isn't it dangerous?'

'It's cold and you have to do what you can. Sometimes life isn't kind. You have a nice place.'

'I don't want you to live on the streets. So please stay here.'

'Thank you. If you are sure? I don't want to get in your way. What about your girlfriend or wife?'

'I'm single. I'm not trying anything on. Trust me, I'm not like that. I just can't see you returning to that world.'

'I'll be back on my feet and I'll pay you back.'

'It's OK, I don't want your money.'

'I don't need charity. I can look after myself.'

'I'm sure you can but it doesn't hurt to accept a helping hand. Remember? I won't ask what has happened. That is your business. A safe roof over your head doesn't hurt in the meantime. Yes?'

Mary approved with a gratifying smile.

'I heard voices?'

'Well it's only me here. I'm doing a kind of diary. A blog.'

'Why?'

'My work.'

'And what is it you do?'

'You look very pale. I have to pop out. Please help yourself to anything. There's some clean clothes in the bedroom. Please stay out of my lab as I am currently running some experiments. I'll get you a front door key so you can come and go as you please.'

'Just until I'm back on my feet, OK?'

'Absolutely.'

Although my previous sermon wasn't as fruitful as I'd wished, I felt I had unfinished business at Speaker's Corner so I returned to further my message and appease my calling. I believed I had secured a regular spot. And after-all I didn't want to disappoint my now fans or followers even if these were by the few. Matt Smith has alot to answer for as bearing my robes I echoed his initial teachings.

'I am no politician. I am not your leader. The power is in your hands. Your actions will resonate through the surviving future populations. You are our saviours! Tell me, what is natural deselection mean to you?!' I hollowed.

'Don't you mean survival of the fittest?' I heard heckled.

'No. That's not the philosophy. Extinction is the loss of attributes. How will you ever become what your bloodline has honoured you with if you cannot follow your destiny? A tree will not reach the sky if it is being suffocated by ivy. We do not need wars and engineered diseases to suppress the population that is not at war with itself in order to survive. Imagine what we could achieve if we turn our backs on irrelevance!' And there she was once more. Stood to the rear of the wandem horde. The lady with the large brimmed summers hat and flowing dress.

'Bravo! It's about time! The theatricals, the message! Right on!' Her voice rang out. And as she removed her hat there was an air of familiarity and also I may say she appeared somewhat distracting to the red blooded male. Although I must admit, I possessed a fetish for women who appear as Victorian prostitutes, this English Rose was having an altogether different effect on me!

'Don't I know you?' I asked.

'Fancy a coffee?'

'Anna?'

I must admit it must have been an unusual sight. The Chosen One, the Messiah sat amongst the proletariat whilst enjoying a beverage. Well, certainly to a group of school kids who took pictures of us on their mobiles. However this was of no concern as despite my composure, I was desperately fighting the urge to the keep my eyes from looking down Anna's top. She was stunning and acting somewhat flirtatious and I was feeling all tingly around her. Was she engaging my subconscious or was I afterall simply a slave to my primeval urges?

'I saw your speeches on the internet and I've been following your blog.'

'It's good to know someone's paying attention. However I feel my words fall upon deaf ears and thus the theatricals.'

'Well maybe you could use some help with your crusade?'

'With all else, I've been spending a lot of focus upon Civil Rights.' This was somewhat untrue. But her help would be certainly be helpful! Maybe even as my first disciple?

'Civil Rights. That's a joke to say the least! It's a delusion to believe we live in a free world. Although we are fortunate enough to not be in a dictatorship, our rights suffer because of the few. Look at The Public Order Act 1984, The Terrorism Act 2000, the Investigatory Powers Act, The Criminal Justice Act and even The Coronavirus Act 2020. Not to mention the Protest Act. Presented with a suspicion the few have taken away our freedom to explore our visions. Murder wouldn't be illegal if we didn't do it or if we didn't object. Understand?'

I certainly shouldn't of treated this book by its cover as this lady was so much more that the one I initially met all those desperate evenings ago.

'Emmeline Pankhurst said 'Freedom or Death but it's hardly the Magna Carta.' I tried to say appearing un-smug.

'The common law principle states, 'Everybody is free to do anything, subject only to the provisions of the law.' Do you think our laws are suffocating us? Ask yourself why are we being persecuted because of the few? And why should we?'

'And I thought you were just a Mental Health Nurse.'

'Comeback to my place Jason and I will teach you about what is hidden from you.'

I asked myself, how could I refuse?!

Anna's place was a well suited town house. A highly polished half grand piano took up the corner of her front room whilst the walls were lined with shelves of books. Anna put on a record, La Taviata (Dammi tu forza! - Give Me Strength) and left the room. I could see this as no ordinary collection as it contained the writings of Nietzsche, Churchill, George Orwell, Karl Marx, John Locke, Plato, Mary Wollstonecraft amongst many others. There were studies of the Druids and next to The Golden Bough was a collection of books about Gigorti Rasputin. Just as I was about to open one as she entered with two glasses of spiced rum on the rocks wearing a rather revealing silk robe.

'Here, try.'

'It's a bit early for me and I don't normally drink'

'Listen to your nurse and drink your medicine. It is good. Sometimes we need to savour our desires not just chase them.'

'Uh, Anna you are well read. Unusual for those I meet.' I nervously said as she seductively responded.

'My favourite, Rasputin. A man of no background, a peasant, an enlightened one who rose to become an influence of a nation. A mystic, a healer and a powerful lover. He couldn't be silenced, he couldn't be killed.' Anna looked deep into my eyes. 'Are you like this man?'

She took me by the hand leading to the Chesterfield sofa.

'Why do you think women were attracted to him?' I asked as she pushed me into the seat and mounted me.

'Perhaps it is the taste of the unknown. Perhaps passion and conviction is the ultimate aphrodisiac. Jason, have you ever made love under a full moon after indulging in mandrake?'

I took a glance at my drink and wondered whether it contained such poison?

'Are we all your puppets?' I timidly asked as if I was her prey about to be devoured.

'It is the flowers that beckons the bees. It is the flowers that controls them.'

Anna pulled me into her cleavage and I'll leave to rest to your imagination. I felt like I was about to be consumed as if caught within her talons or a Venus Fly Trap but what could I do!

Later that afternoon I finally reached home after summoning the strength to break free from Anna's lair! But something didn't feel right as I entered my house.

'Mary? Mary?' I called out.'

There she was, sat on the floor shaking in the corner.

'Mary, what's wrong? Are you OK?' Obviously not!

'I need you to help me...' She nervously replied.

'What's the matter with you? Do you need an ambulance?'

'Lock me in a room and don't let me out.'

'What?! I'm calling an ambulance.'

'I don't need a bloody ambulance! I just need your help.'

'What's the matter with you?'

'Isn't it obvious?! I'm a junky! Please, I'm begging you. Just do what I say. I'll be OK.'

I did what I could only assume was right by holding her. I'm sure this might alleviate her trauma?

'I'll be OK. Don't let me out until at least tomorrow morning. I'll be OK. Thank you. I just need to get straight.'

'What do you need?'

'A bucket, and towels. Water, soup and some pain killers.'

'Who did this to you?'

'Jason, please don't let me out.'

Gathering her to her feet, I then carried her to my bedroom. Mary fell asleep. I locked the window, hid the key and placed her requirements where they could be close to hand. For some subconscious reason I played La Travatan softly on the CD player hoping it to be a pleasant distraction.

'I'm here for you my angel. Just rest. The music might sooth your anxiety?' I whispered down her ear before locking her in by jamming a broom handle against the door handle.

Despite Mary's current circumstances, I couldn't let it disrupt my work. Afterall I was tasked with saving humanity and such a calling could not be shied away from. My sermon had to be uploaded to the blog along with an introduction.

'Hope, will and inspiration are powerful words. Without action these are fruitless. Even to remain dormant until the right time. I can only be your catalyst. We are all our saviours.'

I thought to myself, the media will act as the tip to our spear! I could imagine the beating of the drums of war however it was closer to home coming from the bedroom.

'Let me out!' Mary's shout's hollowed down the hallway. And I had to remain strong for her as if a parent administering tough love.

'Let the poison leave your system my angel.' I calmly advised.

'Don't preach to me you little prick! Let me out!'

'Would you like something to eat?'

'FXXK off!' She replied in a manner unfitting to her or anyone else I must suggest.

'Who did this to you? What about your parents? Should I let them know Mary?'

All went quiet and I pressed my ear against the door. There were no indications of harmful activity so I proceeded to the kitchen to make dinner.

I often found with menial tasks they often inspired the greatest philosophies. Chopping onions always reminded me of the layers within us and society before a bare truth is revealed. Meat as basic and frail as our physical form. Veg? Maybe Anna was correct. We are all the subjects cultivated by vegetation? The distorted reflection against the knife's blade could suggest a distorted vision we share or within our souls.

'I didn't mean what I said. Please let me out Jason. I'm sorry...'

Was this Mary speaking or the beast's persuasion? I thought to myself, is this is a test? A barrier to fate? Retribution? Is she the ivy suffocating my tree? Should she get close? Is the knife tempting me? I blocked her requests out of my head and replacing them with the music La Taviata remembering her as the distracted angel in church smiling at me from the choir.

Some time later diner was ready, so removing the broom handle I entered the bedroom cautiously. There lied Mary, not looking her finest and the room smelled worse that Satan's underpants but at least she was here and safe. I thought it best to clean away the vomit and remove the bucket of urine and other such delights! I placed some flowers beside her bed with a glass of water and her dinner. Replacing the towels and buckets I kissed her upon her forehead and left.

My sermons were yet incomplete, so the following morning demanded a further education for the unenlightened, naturally sporting the robes of justice!

'We are very lucky to be born on this landmass. We don't have to forage for food, fuel or clean water. It's all delivered to our doorsteps. The stores overflow with abundances. Guns are outlawed. Our government supports for us should we fall on bad times and health. We live in a utopia. With every brightness there is a balance. There is a cancer eating away at our potential. We still live in fear. Murder, rape, drugs, abuse, thieves and deceivers suppressing our races' potential! These are the enemies of your evolution. There are more of us than them. There is an exodus from this tyranny. Open your eyes and watch for the burning beacon!'

After preaching my word at further venues before being moved on, I felt my message would finally be out into the world and all thanks to the spectators and their perversion or obsession with mobile phone filming and social media. Although social media disgusted me, where the majority would rather film a person suffering than aid them, on this occasion I thanked them. 'Thank you for making my message easier to publish to the masses I raved!'

'Give Me Strength' or La Traviata had become a contagious theme tune. From Anna to me to Mary. Hopefully inspiring rather than polluting. As I got home I saw the broom lying on the floor with the bedroom door open. I'm sure Houdini would be proud of her. I heard Mary's sweet humming of our contagious tune from the shower. Was she back in action I wished?

'Mary? Mary? Are you OK?'

'I'll be out in a minute.'

'It's OK. Take all the time you need. Would you like some lunch?'

'Thanks for the flowers.'

'No problem.'

My wish has come true as a refreshed Angel appeared in the kitchen wearing a white dressing gown with a towel wrapped round her head. This was certainly the lady I had come to love far from the poor soul discovered surviving on the streets.

'I can't tell you how good that feels.'

'How do you take it?'

'Black with honey.'

'Feeling better?'

'Also, I can't thank you enough for what you have done for me Jason. I'm really sorry if I upset you with anything I might have said.'

'It's OK. I think I understand.'

'You have a nice place. What do you do?'

'I acquired a little luck with my inheritance lets say.'

'What do you do?'

'You might think I'm a bit of a scientist.'

'Thats funny. Me too. I studied organic chemistry at Uni. Where did you go?'

'Uh, just off to the park.'

'Is there a medieval or sci-fi convention there? No, I meant to study?'

'I didn't. Einstein believed you start learning after education. So I skipped the middle man.'

'I hope you aren't suggesting I'm stupid! What's your field of study?'

'Let me show you. How about a field trip?'

'Jason, is your robe something to do with it? Are auditioning for the part of a Jedi or a post apocalyptical profit? Why are you dressed like that Jason?'

'These aren't my normal clothes I assure you.'

At a baron coastline, where waste littered the shore amongst a burnt out wreck of a car is where I led her. This place was reminiscent of a apocalyptical world.

'Jason. Why are we here?' Mary asked.

'That's a very philosophical question however it's away from the prying eyes of the public.'

'What are you intending? And what's in your bag?'

'Nothing to be concerned with right now. Don't worry. I'm not a serial killer.'

'A bit a different at best but in danger I'm very much doubt!' She said in jest.

'Well, this is as good as spot as any. Close your eyes or look away.'

'Are you a drag artist Priscella Queen of the Dump?!'

To which I ignored as I set up the small test rocket. Mary giggled before staring out to sea perhaps longing to be elsewhere. Her hair gently flowed in the breeze.

'You can turn round now.' As if a birthday surprise.

'It's a toy rocket right?' Mary poised.

'No it's an experiment. It's also making a point. So give me a countdown from 5 please.'

'5, 4, 3, 2, 1'

'Firing!' I shouted!

The rocket ignited and shot up into the air before deploying its parachute and gently descending.

'Right. Lets retrieve the little bugger.'

'Jason, what is the point of this?'

'Although the maths and the physics have already been done, I am a strong believer in innovation being a layman's crusade. A bit like Mike Hughes.'

'What?'

'Basically, I want to launch a rocket into space carrying a payload.'

'A missile?' She said looking somewhere between concerned and bewildered.

'No. A vessel. The rocket is merely a taxi to transport it.'

'Isn't NASA and the Chinese already doing this?'

'We cannot afford all of our eggs in one basket. Can we really afford exclusion from the wannabe elite? It's not about sending a payload. It's about sending a message. Well, and the payload.'

As we collected the 'taxi' and dismantling it to fit in my bag, Mary turned to me with a smirk.

'I think you're gonna need a bigger rocket!'

I think she was paraphrasing a line from the film Jaws!

'And there lies the challenge! Lunch?'

Little did she know that our venture to this mighty fine paradise would result in a picnic as I took out sandwiches from my backpack. I was hoping in the back of my mind this could be some kind of date and I passed her a nearby flower. After all she had been a part of my world from the offset. Could she be part of my world from now on? Time is short and my motives had doubled.

'In chaos there is always beauty.' I gently whispered.

She placed the Sea Pink behind her ear as if accepting my courting gestures. I felt like Lord Byron was guiding me.

'Why are you being so good to me? I don't deserve it. You've done enough.'

'Look around. In desolation there is hope. What are your plans? Can you go back to your parents? They could help you.'

What was I saying? Was I trying to push her away after beckoning her? Or was my subconscious acting as insidious? I was simply trying to come across as honourable rather than desperate.

'Jason. Do you know why cross pollination is important?' Mary asked whilst examining the flower's petals.

'Mary?' Where was this leading I thought. Was this goddess now beckoning me?

'It strengthens the gene. Taking on the attributes of another to survive and evolve.'

'I don't always see it like that. Like people. Where demand or population is at its greatest, it begins to feed upon itself. Again to survive but not evolve. Degrading the gene. Maybe sometimes a fire is needed for the sake of purification?'

'Or a cull!'

'Precisely.'

Mary laughed. I believe I was being led down the mocking path.

'Jason, I always thought you were a unique and crazy boy. You sound like a Bond villain.'

'Is it delusional to think of oneself as our saviour?'

'I'm not sure how scientific that sounds. More like something from the Church. However I'm interested to know more. So my answer to your proposal is yes!'

'Marriage?'

'No, your aid, yes?'

'Can I trust you?'

'It's simply a matter of having faith in me. So take that first step!'

And with that we sat there a little longer in silence looking out to the horizon.

That night my dreams spoke to me. Upon a cliff's edge Mary and I stood hand in hand. It seemed the cosmos stood still as we could feel the Earth's rotation. As the night's sky turned to ultraviolet I turned to her.

'Our senses only bear witness to that which is before us but there is so much more.'

The weaving pattern of background cosmic radiation danced upon her enchanted eyes.

Allowing Mary into my laboratory was a kin to allowing her into my mind and soul, where I had already considered she resides. Paraphrasing my nurse, now you will become far, far away from the maddening crowd and yet enlightened to what must be. As if entering Solomon's Mines, Mary wide opened eyed walked around my lab, looking at the ideas upon the whiteboards, the rocket prototypes, the biospheres, my pet octopus, Darwin and finally came upon the board featuring 'PROJECT EXODUS.'

'What is all of this?'

'I believe we can be led away from our perspective of self destruction to a better world. Quite simply and ultimately, I aim to seed other habitual environments in the cosmos whilst aid evolution here on Earth.'

'Exodus? Do you see yourself as Moses? Who is this for? Are you being paid?'

'Financial reward is irrelevant and this is a necessity. Like every revolution needs a leader, every project needs a title.'

'So how far have you got?'

'Well, getting close to applying practice to theory.'

'Experimenting? Results? Perhaps your need of help couldn't of come sooner.'

The silence of our mutual content was broken with the doorbell making Mary nervously jump to the point where she dropped her bag and her mobile phone fell out.

'It's OK. You're safe. No one knows you're here. It's probably just a delivery. Why don't you pop the kettle on?'

Mary left the lab leaving her phone and bag on the floor. Perhaps her mind was elsewhere? And as I went to answer the door. The image of my younger self crossing the river using the stepping stones came to mind. Perhaps all our minds are elsewhere and always have been?

On entering the kitchen Mary had made me a lovely steaming cup of herbal tea. Her face was somewhat changed from bewilderment in the lab, to numbness. Vacantly staring out the window. I thought a distraction might help.

'Mary, how do you see time?'

'Passing very quickly.'

'As we sit here I see myself in the future looking back.'

'Tell me more.'

'Well, the tasks I have to forfill later. Once complete I will be looking back as a matter of cause and effect. Leading onwards to the next stepping stone. This is why I believe in fate. It is your future self looking back at the line of events that lead you there.'

'Perhaps that's why I'm here? I need to be near you. I need you to support me. I can't return to that world. Perhaps it is a sign, a path. Looking back, is this fate? What does the future hold when I look back.'

'Tell me what happened.'

'I used to believe in life, liberty, learning.'

'Love?'

'Not anymore.'

'What happened?'

'My boyfriend became a junky. And it wasn't long before he owed a lot of money. When he couldn't pay his debts he let his dealer pay off the interest. But with me.'

'With you?'

It was at this point my imagination pictured Mary being pushed against her will into her bedroom by these Satanic beasts. The door left ajar whilst her lover began jacking up to the sound of her tortured screams.

Putting aside the idea my angel suffered a boyfriend that wasn't I, my ideology of hope descended into the realisation of utter disgust. How can these walking animals of filth soil my angel of resurrection. I had never before felt such mounting rage claw itself from my insides out. My thoughts turned to the justice only rage can offer. Castrate the rapists was too subtle to rebalance the equation. But what could I do was the question that would haunt me. This could be my Darkest Hour?

Mary continued: 'They didn't stop and he did nothing so I ran away. I had no-one and the streets seemed to be safer. They were anonymous where I could hide. And that's where I met you.'

'And what about the police? Your parents?'

'The police? With junkies there is no case for them. My Parents?! And how could I tell my parents? FXXking animals! Vince and Darren. I want them dead!!'

'You have to report them. Your Dad can help? He's not just a priest. He's your father.'

'He cares more of his standing than me. Behind closed doors life is never what is appears. I wished I was dead.'

With a deep breath and a heavy heart I could only advise Mary such:

'Dead?! That would have been an insult to those who survived the wars, famine, diseases and nature's revenges with you here today. And the gratitude of those in the future who's existences depend on your survival.'

'Right?' And with a realisation of hope Mary began to clear her tears.

'Perhaps life wants more from you. Perhaps your future lineage needs you more than you currently know...' I calmly presented.

That night I suffered what I hoped was a vision upon my slumber. I saw an urban underpass. I saw a gang of Hoodies smoking drugs and drinking spirits. Poor un-enlightened discards of humanity. I witnessed their behaviour as if they were a rotten horde of hyaenas becoming self ingested. Like a holy messiah ordained in a long white robe I entered the devils pit as if wilfully becoming their lamb to be slaughtered. Their growls, their barks became distant as I passed. Removing my hood to gaze upon the cosmos the gang's screams became muted as they melted like candles. What was my vision's meaning and what path should be walked I asked myself? Well isn't it obvious!

Entering my lab I picked up Mary's mobile phone and address book from her bag. I found the contacts for her parents, her boyfriend and Vince. All that was now required was ofcourse a beautiful plan. One of sorts was beautifully brewing.

As my projects developed so would my need for an increase in working space. And within this one horse town I thought of only one who had two! Although my landlord Farmer Tyler didn't like people I felt this was beyond a social engagement and our species' necessity demanded such. Being a good tenant I paid him a visit.

Cautiously walking down the lane to the farm house I could see him stumbling around the forecourt whilst brandishing a bottle of whiskey and a rifle.

'Who goes there!' He hollowed aiming the rifle in my direction.

'Tyler? It's me Jason. Your tenant.' Raising my hands as if to surrender.

'And what do you bloody well want?!'

'To give you more money!'

He pondered for a second before lowering the rifle.

'For what?'

'I'm engineering a rocket and require an outhouse to construct it.'

'A rocket?'

'Yes. I aim to save the world.'

'Flash Gordon! You mad bastard! How can one deny such eccentricity?!'

'Were you going to shoot me?'

'I only shoot ramblers and dog walkers with this tranquilliser gun. They are all a bunch of trespassing bastards! Breaking my fences, my signs, leaving litter and hanging their dog shit bags on my gates posts. And worse of all answering back after I tell them to get the fXXk off my land!!'

'Well, I won't be in the way. I work alone. No people, no noise. You'll hardly know I am here at all. I'm sure your wife would like some extra cash?'

'My wife? What do you know of her?.'

'Nothing...'

'I have no wife, well not anymore. I imagine you heard the gossip? What a bitch! Well, she died in a freak yachting accident leaving me to look after all this by myself!'

'Sorry, I didn't know, anything.'

'Those pricks in the village sticking knifes in my back again?'

'I don't know anyone in the village.'

'Well, do you have an outbuilding I could use? How much would you like?'

'We'll work something out.'

Tyler staggered into the farmhouse leaving his rifle leant up against the tractor. And with that my plan's initiation commenced!

JUST POPPED OUT. BACK SOON.
X

Was the note I left for Mary as I ventured into the night to commence my act of righteous justice. Returning later when all was quite and Mary was asleep, I placed the holdall and tranquilliser gun away in the back of the cupboard hidden behind some boxes. I hoped my late night shower wouldn't wake her. It was vitally important she didn't discover any evidence that could support a conviction for my acts.

'Jason? It's the middle of the night. Are you OK?' Mary asked.

'Fine thanks?'

'Where have you been? It's very late.'

'Fancied a bit of fresh air whilst all is quite. Just to clear my head. Sorry if I woke you.' I said calm and convincingly.

'OK. I'm going back to bed. Do you want a drink?'

'No thanks, I'm fine.'

To proceed once more with a sense of normality.

As I lied on my sofa I remembered my 10th birthday with just Mum, Dad and me.

'Blow out the candles and make a wish Jason.' Mum said with a smile.

'Remember, keep your wish a secret and it'll come true.' Dad joined in with.

Not wholly convinced extinguishing these candles utilising my exhaling breath would make my dreams a reality I still proceeded to keep them happy. I believed my dreams were my inevitable destiny so their reality would come into fruition which ever path I took.

'Presents!' Dad excitedly announced.

Nevertheless tell me someone who isn't excited when offered cake and gifts. Dad passed me a medium sized box which I eagerly tore the wrapping off. I was half expecting a rocket or remote control car however I received a microscope. Was this one of Dad's lessons I assumed as he fetched some pre-prepared slides? He placed them into the microscope offering it to me.

'Jason. Tell me what you see?'

Peering into the eye piece I played with the lenses and focused to attain a closer observation.

'I see movement. Is it tiny creatures?'

'Everything we see in life is created by smaller things. If we understand the little cogs in life, we can understand the makings of everything else. Maybe even influence them. An understanding of this is the understanding of fate.' Dad advised.

Maybe no-one truly understands the world of quantum but this gift represented organics. Maybe a little much for a birthday present however his lessons far outranked anything a train-set could offer!

'Dad? Where did these come from?' I asked inquisitively.

'Earwax!' Dad replied like an excited school boy.

'John!' Mum was less impressed and passed me a present containing a jumper, socks and pants.

I believe the recall of this memory was to serve as a reminder to the gravity that we all choose to become as well as perhaps my destiny being guided.

The following morning I set to work in the lab with an experiment by mixing the gases of nitrogen and methane under a ultraviolet light. Sealing the mixture to become a further biosphere. This was my experiment with both creation and to illuminate how simply our origins once were and perhaps simulate the direction life could evolve whilst in different environments. Perhaps mimicking those performed on Spacelab? For example how would our cells develop on a different world in terms of atmospheric chemistry and the influence of its gravity?

Mary brought me a cup of tea and a couple of biscuits.

'Have you been to bed?' She asked.

'Ofcourse. Just a lot to do.'

'You know you can have your room back.'

'I'm an early riser and I don't wish to disturb you. The sofa is fine.'

'What are you doing? Creating organic compounds?'

'Mary, while you are there, could you feed Darwin for me?'

I had a slight thought that perhaps Darwin with his nine brains was observing us.

'Well today this experiment and questioning on the necessity for predators?'

'Within an ecosystem ofcourse. Otherwise it wouldn't self manage resulting in the system's extinction. No plants, no herbivores, no carnivores. You can't have one without the other. They all evolve together.' Mary so wisely advised.

'And what about omnivores? Humans lets say. Do we need to be cultivated? Should we prey upon ourselves?' I was trying not to ask leading questions only to gather an idea as to where her mental standing resided.

'I'm not sure where you're leading?'

'Well, is it a necessity that we turn on each other?'

'Survival has no morals. It's cruel and dictates. If we can't trade then we take? And those who house the greatest warriors and maybe the lowest morals wins, yes?'

'And for pleasure? What about greed? Is it true, given the chance, a lamb doesn't stop suckling?'

'I don't know?' Mary replied with a degree of intrigue.

'Well, if it's not for a species' welfare and simply greed, is this not a crime against its own purpose? A selfish act maybe? Not a necessity? Should it be punished?'

'By who? Maybe a specific example might help?'

'Do you believe the punishment should fit the crime? What about an 'Eye for an Eye?'

'An 'Eye for an Eye leaves the World blind.' If you are referring to people, then I'd like to think the person we are today differs from yesterday. People's yesterdays or regrets might not be their future achievements.

'Interesting thanks.'

'Um, your welcome?'

I hoped I hadn't confused her as to my true intentions or justification for them.

Farmer Tyler's outbuilding had finally found its use however not precisely what I originally planned for it. I didn't think Tyler would worry when I borrowed 2 of his lambs for this particular experiment. On entering the barn I was pleased to see my test subjects hadn't managed to escape as they were still bound to their chairs back to back, blindfolded and gagged. And ofcourse naked. I had been playing a mixture of white noise and screams down their headphones serving as sense depredation and torture. Perhaps the hurt they have caused others now returned to haunt them? Righteousness? Justice? I removed their headphones to advise them of such:

'Ask yourself how a man can die better? Ask yourself who are the tyrants and what is the temple of our Fathers and Gods. What will you do when facing the invading hordes? Do you believe the punishment should fit the crime?' A tad contrived I admit.

And with this I applied the lambs to their instruments of rape. And left them to it.

Locking the barn doors I had a gentle ponder imagining a tree falling silently in the woods.

If we dispose of the criminals against evolution then you inevitably become that which you champion to extinguish. The murderer of murderers, the poisoner of propaganda. This is why our acts have to be justified as a necessary truth for survival. A Reality Revolution.

Lying on my sofa I was contemplating the morality of my actions towards the two rapists. Was I justified in my methods? Should I have performed such an act? And what happens now with them? I am no murderer so perhaps I should set them free? I could imagine this act of mercy becoming a hurdle to future efforts such as their retribution. My thoughts moved to the biosphere experiments looking at the origins to create a better more adapt species.

'Sorry Jason, I just needed to get a glass of water and I saw your light on. Can't sleep?'

'Ah, 'to sleep and perchance to dream...'

'And what would you dream of?'

'Perhaps the perfect being.'

'Being?'

'When I was a boy I drew a picture. I believe I still have it.'

'Show me.'

How could I deny such enthusiasm. So I jumped up in search of my masterpiece! Foraging in old boxes of research notes.

'I thought we are limited by our own current senses as well as physicality.

We see between 430 to 790 THz. We hear between 20hz to 20KHz. This is only a fraction of the frequency range. Then there is smell, touch and taste. What about sense of balance, gravity, electromagnetism, sonar, pressure and spacial. Perhaps time and that which is about to happen. Like being in a still pool and a pebble is dropped at the far end. The ripples resonate like energy through space time. And ofcourse the ability to self replace or change form. Oh, also, like the Immortal Jelly fish, the ability to reverse its life cycle. Here it is.'

I handed Mary the old folded crayon image. A cross between human, dolphin, octopus, shark and reptile. As Mary looked at it somewhat amused I momentarily pictured her head upon the body of my creation.

'Are we all on experiments upon your Island, Dr Moreau?' She said in jest.

Mary poured herself a glass of water ruffled my head and returned to bed.

At this point my mind turned to an early influence, Mike Hughes performing this world record breaking Limo jump. I thought to myself...

Anything is possible if you have the will. I would have loved to met him and witnessed his rocket launch. Obviously not the fatal one.

5.

THE PAYLOAD.

My story doesn't always follow an assumed timeline as our thoughts and recollections often jump from one relevance to the next rather than being cognitive.

Some time before Mary re-entered my life, turning theory into practice required set up. Not all the equipment I demanded for my experiments and engineering projects could be easily attained over the internet or retail outlets without arousing unwanted attention. So I had no option but to get creative. The nearest university hosted a well stocked Physics and Engineering Departments and it would be there I could benefit greatest.

Halloween offered the perfect opportunity. So during a students party I disguised myself as Frankenstein's monster pushing an old patient trolley hosting the shape of a body underneath a sheet. I had written in fake blood 'Mary Shelley' on the linen for added comic effect. A perfect camouflage for the occasion whilst presenting an apt statement. Pacing the car park I drew closer to the buildings under the suggestion my presence was part of the evening's events, eventually becoming an accepted part of the scenery.

This was a great strategy to gain entrance to the target area as well as being an adrenaline thrill on a scale I was otherwise unused to. When all had settled down and I was no longer of interest to the students as to whom my true identity was, I would make my move to the Physics and Engineering Department. Ofcourse these places would be both locked and alarmed, as their treasures were not of a cheap nature. The beauty of the trolley was the tools I had just carried unseen past the security and staff were to aid me gaining entrance as well as concealing the equipment I so desperately sought. With regards to the alarms, my thoughts were if you can't disable them then create more to smother them. So using the students as cover and daring on my side, I would hit the fire alarm. The responding Emergency Services would initially attend to them whilst I broke into where I needed to be and in the ensuing chaos I could make my hasty escape into the shroud of the darkness. At least when reviewing any CCTV footage the following day they could say Frankenstein's monster did it!

'Who dares wins!' Hats off to the SAS's moto for their inspiration of will. All was successfully achieved. My only regret was feeling remorse for the students who actually used the equipment that I had just acquired. For it isn't my intention to deny them theirs. I did however contemplate, it's not theft if it's in the service to save us. However I must admit I have become a master at my game!

My garden shed had became a makeshift observatory where I received, examined and searched for hidden messages from the cosmos. Being a bit like S.E.T.I (The Search of Extraterrestrial Intelligence.) I must admit with no luck! I used the University's inadvertently borrowed laser to broadcast binary communications about us to the stars. A bit like Carl Sagan's Golden Disc upon the Voyagers but without the need of transportation and a record player! While monitoring the equipment I would often imagine a clear blue sky featuring my three Neutron Stars. As if those upon Orion's Belt, Alnitak, Alnilam, and Mintaka. I would observe them and consequently see me upon a planet alien to us with these three being its suns. I would look down and see my hands with longer fingers and an extra set of thumbs.

I would imagine a distant planet with a red sky receiving my laser broadcast featuring Carl's hydrogen based coding and its message of DNA to human. How would they interpret this message? A design or maybe a delicious recipe?

As with the Golden Disc, my reasoning shouldn't be constrained to the internet becoming lost amongst the volume from those polluting the airwaves with messages of irrelevance, so I would also broadcast my blogs, my sermons to outer space. Was it wishful thinking to believe whether anyone out there was paying attention?

As I reviewed my recent post I considered how alien my messages might appear to those out there let alone those here?

'It's no secret that my love of humanity is somewhat non-existent. But in the light of the out-ruling Neanderthals questioning my reasoning, let this be my continued testament. With every passing moment the Universe is expanding. It's accelerating and leaving us behind. The longer left the closer we are to exclusion and extinction.'

Imagine a Polar Bear swimming out to a shoreless sea with desperate hope. Our mortal coil cannot survive the distances to reach the next habitable planet. And our planet cannot survive the greed of us. Picture an apple being consumed by maggots. So my plan is thus. Extend ourselves up there whilst save our lives here.'

As bleak as it sounds, there is hope. So let's focus on the initial.

The Theory:

Sat in the Lab, I was observing my Octopus, Darwin. I imagined what he might be thinking surrounded by whiteboards and images of the giants such as Nicola Tesla,

Einstein, Plato and Davinci to mention but a mere few. He was a true blue blooded nine brained wonder of existence, that could communicate and shape-shift. I wondered if he would of liked to of read 'The Origin of Species.' He might see its studies as being obvious without giving its concepts any further thought.

'Probably all organic beings which have ever lived on this Earth have descended from some primordial form, into which life was first breathed.' Darwin would advise.

Picturing the atomic to the cuttlefish would he question whether this a natural progress or a wonderful accident? From energy, to mass, to merger. Amino acids to proteins to cells. That's all we are. A string of cognitive building blocks where one triggers the next. I think my octopus would look upon Michel Angela's 'Vitruvian Man' as a lesser more farcical being than itself. Imagine the cognitive beauty of it. An Amoeba to Jellyfish, to fish, to mud-skipper to reptile to bird diving into the waves. An organic form developed as per it's survival demands. Imagine the Jellyfish. Nothing more than a length of nerves and a stomach. Simply reacting. Coil the nervous system and a brain is formed to cross communicate. Further than simple nerve reactions comes the development of thought, and memory, resulting in consciousness. 'I think therefore I am.' But where do we find instinct and can this be designed? Is there more? What am I missing? Is it like Michel Angelo's painting of The Creation of Adam? Are we engineered rather than being circumstantial or accidental? How could this be replicated? Could our form be 3D printed? Could memory be encoded as instinct? And from each beginning a vast leap of evolution could commence with hereditary instinct becoming hereditary memory. Somewhere between the 4 letters comprising the DNA code hides this secret. Perhaps it's like binary? Where it's either zero or one however with a larger combination presenting a viable? And once established we can form a gathered knowledge bank, exponential with its input and able to be exported.

After-all, how does a spider construct a web or a bee a hive?

I spend a lot of time deliberating the DNA coding mystery without nature revealing her secrets. A diary / blog entry might prevent me from pulling my hair out with frustration! Can I let one study area prevent progress overall I ask myself?

'I am having problems identifying where hereditary instinct resides within the DNA structure. Not that I'm either a geneticist or biologist. From my research, it simple doesn't make any sense. This is what has held me back. Rather than spending a lifetime of potential unsuccessful research within trial and error, if the cell contains all from the original then it is the contemporary cell and DNA that is our seed. To seed a distant habitual zone with a primordial soup containing my DNA is the payload. AKA Panspermia.'

'Venturing back to the original cell, it's a series of switches to instructing the cells what task needs to be forfilled. Our mutation is still in motion as per the demands for its survival.' I thought Darwin was advising. The octopus ofcourse, not the ghost of the legend. Otherwise you might think I have lost my mind!

'Perhaps we could map our physical evolution as per environmental demands then adapt this method for differing worlds?'

I thanked Darwin for his input whilst picturing the classic image of an Ape walking to become Man. And a then Man then becoming something more.

Continuing my fitness regime the following morning I went for a jog to the park. And there upon a bench whilst catching my breath I observed ants feeding upon the litter from an overflowing bin and like normal all observations and experiences I believed were part of my fate to save our species. On this occasion I thought to myself:

We can't send a person but we can send a payload. Create the fitting species upon arrival. Afterall our form is forever in a transient state of development. Is there really a human state? We originated from scavengers surviving on the protein remains of brains and bone marrow.

Can you imagine Michelangelo's Vitruvian Man but with the body of a Cephalopod?

Even though I was 'The Chosen One', I felt a tad daunted with the tasks I was cursed with. A man is not an octopus! With a mere single brain and only one pair of hands, I am somewhat limited. And time is our enemy. My vision demands more cogs. Observing the co-ordination of the ants gave me an idea. I need to recruit those of upmost intellect and action, who were able to work under secrecy. Those who shared my vision bearing their own crusade for survival. As an ode to the invented of the computer, Alan Turin and the code breakers at Bletchley Park I put a question out there.

CAN SUPERMAN FLY?
PROVE IT TO WIN A PRIZE.
#LEGACY

Until I or my future colleagues could brake the DNA code, for the moment my conclusion to the DNA issue remained simply. There is no human, there is only the cell. And that will be my initial payload. The seed.

6.
THE GREAT ESCAPE

Was it the act of Steve McQueen jumping the fence on the motorbike that made it dramatic or was it the fact of everything leading up to this point is what made it so? The plan, the tools, the tunnelling, and the sheer audacity that made that moment a pinnacle?

Remaining content with the initial payload it is time to leap the next boundary, gravity. Keeping in mind it took NASA a rocket the size of 110.6 metres weighing at 6.2 million pounds simply to launch 3 men to the moon with their baggage. I just need to launch a vial. The single cell of my

DNA. Comprising from elements from the beginning of our universe.

Transporting this will be inventive as I have no access to the future of propulsion. Entanglement, Ion drives, space warping, gravitational surfing, laser sailing or worm holes amongst all the other future designs. My current theory is thus, once escaping Earth's gravitational hold, perpetual motion is our key. Newton put it best in his First Law of Motion.

'An object in motion tends to stay in motion unless an external force acts upon it.'

The problem is this. I don't believe the authoritative powers will permit use of their utilities or services. So in the spirit of the just, it is left to me. To break gravity and attain perpetual motion I need to reach to Karmin line that borders Earth from space. This is only 100km straight up. Then ofcourse the rest of planetary gravity with a velocity of 11.2 km per second. A further 300 miles to clear our planet's gravity? Achieving this would be easy if I could beg, borrow or steal from the higher powers.

I can't see either Branson, Bezos or Musk helping, more over them hijacking Project Exodus.

If I could use NASA's High Altitude Research Project (HARP Supergun). I could simply fire the payload into space or utilise a launch platform.

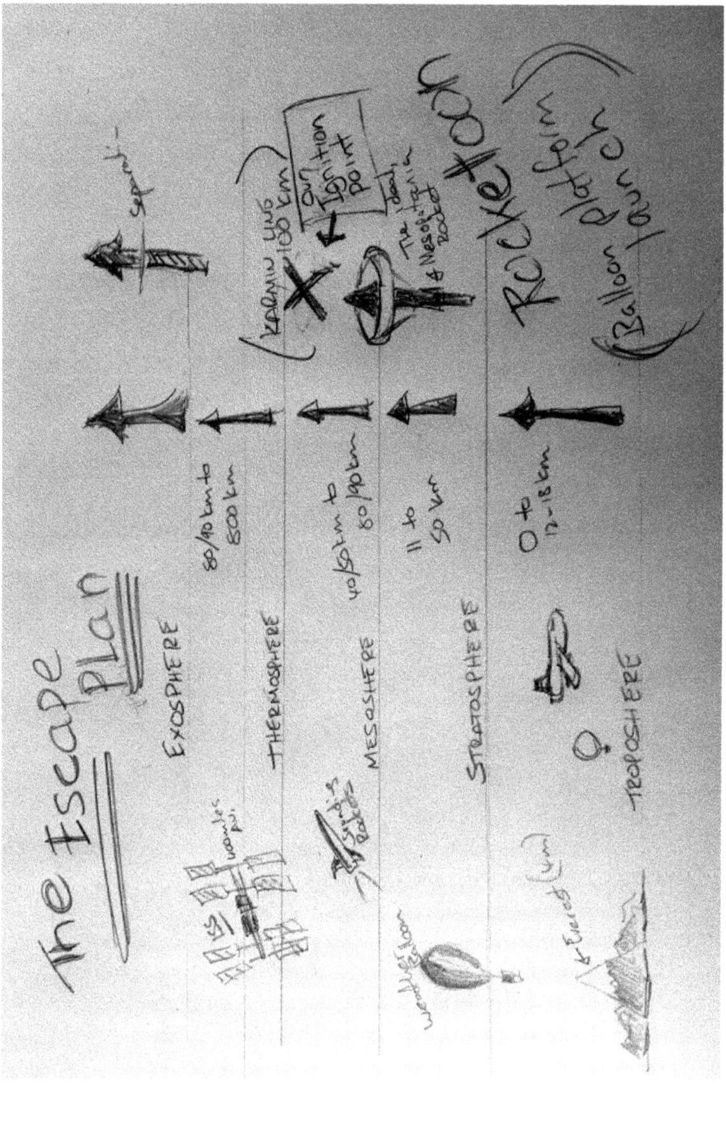

Lets put this into perspective. Everest is 8.8km high. And the highest a self made rocket has flown is 116 KM. So there are solutions if only such resources to attain this were currently feasible. However I have no alternative but to find a solve this. Even if initial attempts prove unsuccessful. I believe my layman's effort will inspire others. Afterall, everyone loves the failures and successes from an underdog. Just look at Eddie the Eagle!

My initial designs would be a conductive casing which absorbed cosmic radiation channelling it into a form of propulsion like a squid moving through water. A bit like a jet. We can only utilise that which is present beyond. Was Frank Whittle thinking about this when he invented the jet engine or was it simply he didn't like propellers?

With a spin induced upon launch from the fins and the nose cone to provide power to the pump and communications.

The Mk.1 'MESOPOTAMIA' Rocket Design.

Beginning with the Nose Cone. This is ridged in opposite direction to the angled fins to create a spin upon launch to drive the internally perpetual motion Mag-Lev engine.

This engine drives the Ionic compressor that funnels background radiation to the chamber until pressure amounts to release a sphincter to the booster. The engine also provides a source of electrical power to the transmitter.

4 glass vials contain the DNA and amino acids payloads are housed at the front encased in gold leaf for protection against cosmic radiation along it providing a degree of insulation.

The rocket's main body is of a conductive and radiation absorbent carbon based material that is both light weight and strong.

The first stage booster is made from cardboard containing a high level of oxygen rich based solid fuel mix where all is consumed upon launch finally revealing the main rocket. It contains the altitude pressure ignition system carrying a pocket of oxygen gas to aid firing in the upper atmosphere.

Initial issues to overcome:

Survivability of organic payload.

Materials durability under extremes of temperatures and pressures.

How much spin is required to produce required energy.

Can Cosmic Background Radiation be an adequate fuel source? Can it be harnessed and can it be compressed?

Separation of booster to Rocket be achieved without causing damage?

Once these designs have proved successful, MK. 2 will contain no moving internal parts to ensure a greater endurance threshold.

——————————-

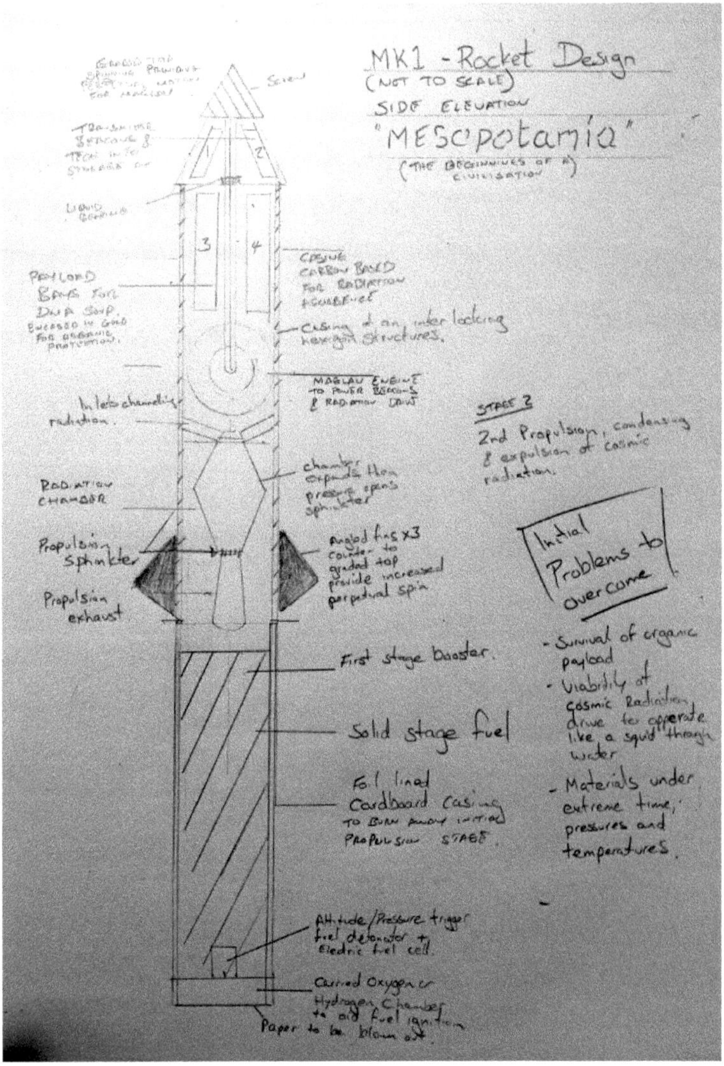
MK1 - Rocket Design
(NOT TO SCALE)
SIDE ELEVATION
"MESOPotamia"
(THE BEGINNINGS OF A CIVILISATION)
Screw
LIQUID BEARING
PAYLOAD BAYS FOR DNA SOUP, ENCASED IN GOLD FOR ORGANIC PROTECTION.
Casing of an interlocking hexagon structures.
MAGLEV ENGINE TO POWER BEACONS & RADIATION DRAW
Inter channelling radiation.
STAGE 2
2nd Propulsion, condensing & expulsion of cosmic radiation.
RADIATION CHAMBER
chamber expands then pressure opens sphinkter
Propulsion Sphinkter
Angled fins x3 counter to graded top provide increased perpetual spin
Propulsion exhaust
Initial Problems to overcome
- Survival of organic payload
- Viability of cosmic Radiation drive to opperate like a squid through water
- Materials under extreme time, pressures and temperatures.
First stage booster.
Solid stage fuel
Foil lined Cardboard Casing TO BURN AWAY INITIAL PROPULSION STAGE.
Altitude/Pressure trigger fuel detonator + Electric fuel cell.
Carried Oxygen or Hydrogen Chamber to aid fuel ignition
Paper to be blown out.

It was at this point Mary popped in.

'I believe in your mission Jason. I believe in you. How can I help?'

Sadly I had to face the truth, my engineering skills would simply not cut the mustard. So an alternative had to be sought.

With a tad of research into universities and rocket clubs I was fortunate to discover one such character who was proud to sport his home-made device and I knew he would have to be paid a visit. However I could not afford an offer being rejected. This is where Mary could assist. This is where she would become both my accomplice and apprentice.

With the tune of Bad News 'Warriors of Gengus Khan' playing in my head and sporting an Einstein mask I broke into his workshop during the dead of the night. Afterall the end justifys the means, right! As the burglar alarms commenced I ran with this 8ft rocket to an awaiting Mary who was my get away driver. Without looking back I heard the shouts of an extremely disgruntled owner.

'Oi!!!'

Mary wore a mask of Emily Pankhurst which might not have been as recognizable as mine. However both were very suited for the occasion I must add!

As I jumped into the vehicle and we sped away Mary shouted out of the window.

'Freedom or death!

Later I could imagine the owner and his wife giving a description to the police.

'Did you get a look at them?' The Policeman would ask.

'Yes, it was Einstein and Emily Pankhurst! They stole my rocket!' The owner would reply in a rather angst and confused manner.

Not being utterly scrupulous, like a great 1970's diamond theft leaving a white glove, I left a note simply reading:

NEEDS MUST. SORRY BUT THANKS,
Yours
WERNER VON BRAUN.

Back at the lab I immediately set to work converting this rocket to cater for our needs. I removed its returning parachute to make space for the payload.

Mary was still exhilarated from the experience.

'What happens now?' She asked.

'We attach the payload encased in gold leaf as a protection against cosmic radiation, into the nose and off we go.'

'I don't wish to sound odd, but what is the difference between what you are doing and what NASA has done with Voyager?'

''The only problem is this will only go about 38 miles which leaves us a tad short. Perhaps boosters? Yes boosters! Sorry did you say something?'

'Uh?' Mary expressed with shrugged shoulders.

'Voyager? Yes? They are sending a greeting. We are sending life. Both however are sending a message. And perhaps our initial efforts in probability will not be successful. It is the first stepping stone. Besides, what about the Voyager paradox?

'I'm sorry Jason, I don't understand?'

'In order for the Golden Disc to survive the traumas of time and space it was coated in uranium. So what ever disco raving alien discovers it, viewing the images, they will initially believe Earthlings are in a constant state of flares and dodgy moustaches. Then, sadly, the degraded uranium could kill them! Is this really a greeting?! It's like a bomb coated in glitter. If it doesn't, imagine if they journey here and try to fit in with this understanding? Can you picture an alien being sat on a bus dressed in the attire of 'glam rock' attempting to assume anonymity?

'And what about the philosophy where a superior species will always enslave or exterminate the lesser?' Mary quite rightly asked.

'Hm... Very good point however what choice do we have?' I ultimately felt the gravity of her point and sat back with this ethical conundrum leering.

'I think we could both do with a break. A change of scene. A spot of normality perhaps?'

Mary and I attending a local Chinese street festival as they celebrated their New Year. It seemed like we were on a date as we observed the traditions with dancing, dragons and firecrackers.

'So all that remains is the launch, yes? The rocket still does not look big enough to reach space.' Said Mary.

'Yes, We are somewhat limited. Engineering the rocket is relatively simply. Obtaining the hydrogen peroxide is something else. You can't just walk into your high street chemist. And being highly volatile apart from the explosive risk it does tend to eat through everything. Our single stage solid fuelled rocket is safer and it will at best reach 30 miles.'

'Even if you were stood on top of Everest it still would not be high enough to reach the Karmin Line. Why don't you make it bigger?'

'Well, to save fuel we need a launch platform to reach more than 60 miles up.'

We found a seat and watched the fireworks.

'And that is where are problem lies.' I advised.

As we shared a drink and opened our fortune cookies. Wishful thinking hoped they contained the message BE MORE! I looked across to see a group of children releasing candle lanterns. They looked magnificent as they ventured into the night's sky with their flickering light. I thought about weather balloons. I thought about an Astronaut performing a space jump to Earth.

'As we get higher the atmosphere becomes thinner and the fuel becomes increasingly efficient.'

With the fireworks, and lanterns Mary and I felt temporarily removed from our quest simply to enjoy the moment. I thought how fortunate I was to be in her presence and how fate was blessing me from the moment we met in church to each of us finding one another once more. It seemed our existences were certainly destined to be entwined. I looked into her eyes and leaned forward to kiss her. She didn't pull away and we equally met. Perhaps this was the moment I thought about those many years ago? Would she bear me a child? It was at this point she leant back and smiled.

'Lets get out of her.' She said seductively. Once again, who was I to say no!

Now back home, Mary led me by the hand to the bedroom. She tore away my clothes like a hungry savage about to devour its prey. She threw me onto the bed and mounted me as if an the untamed banshee. As her soft breasts beat me about my face I thought of the weather helium balloons once more. Helium! As balloons get higher they expand. 10 times!

'Yes, yes, then thrust! We can do it!'

'Do it to me Jason! Thrust me. Thrust me!' Mary cried out.

Ignition within a thinner atmosphere. 1952! James Van Allen! Rocket, balloon. I thought during our rampage.

'Rockoon! Yes! Panspermia!!' I cried out as she stole my innocence. She had taken my cherry as I had taken the rocket. The exhilaration was extreme. I hoped she felt the same way too. I hope she wasn't faking it!

The following morning was like no other as I awoke next to my dream woman. My saving grace, my Mary Magdalene. She was like an inspiration in the lab, a Robin hood in the field and a Victorian prostitute in my bed. What more would a gentleman want for I ask? So I thought I'd treat her with a full slap up English breakfast at a cafe bordering the city.

It had seemed as she had cemented our relationship with the previous evening's performance. I didn't eat much as all I could do was admire her whilst ignoring life outside of the window. Mary must have been ravenous as she ate hers before starting on mine. I thought it rude to continue to ogle her as she feasted so grabbing a napkin I sketched the ideal launch cradle for the rocket.

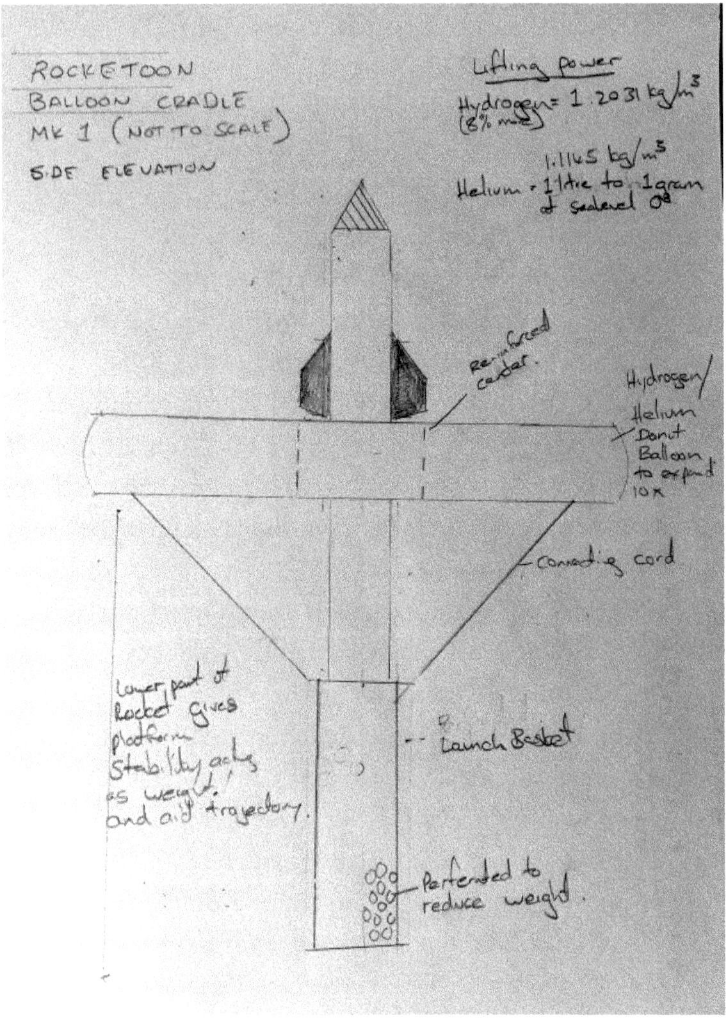

'I could eat for the two of us.' Mary momentarily advised with a slurp of tea. I didn't want to suggest she was as this might be misconstrued. So I tried to remain engaged upon our work.

'Like a Weather Balloon but doughnut shaped for the rocket to launch through cradled in a mount. Helium as the inert gas.'

'I'm pleased for you.'

'All of which are feasibly attainable.' I muttered.

'About last night...'

'Yes pleased? I love you.'

'You love me?' Mary questioned.

Although last night fate was in my favour, today it must be taunting me. Is this the universal equilibrium that came with a knock on the window? Who was this scabby looking fool?

'Keith?' Mary looked taken back.

'Do you know him?' I asked.

'My ex. Sorry Jason.' She rose out of her chair and hurried outside. And for a second time I felt hate brewing inside me, clawing to get out. The animal was stirring!

As Keith attempted to greet her with open arms I was glad to see she welcomed him with a slap in the face and a knee to his privates! They began one of those interesting street arguments which I was trying to avoid hearing. I quietly rehearsed my later words to Mary.

'Love you? Yes. I always have...'

7.
VIVA LA REVOLUTION!!

I found myself staring at a fried egg. Although this was essentially the aftermath of a chicken's period, to me it represented so much more. In content the proteins and yoke being the beginnings of life and in metaphor, the sun, the earth and the cosmos reaching out and in form, breakfast! I considered my mission, to extend life up there and yet ensure life down here. As Earth is our lifeboat, I believed I should now focus on shoring it up.

Trust me I hadn't forgotten about our two guests unwilfully residing at the farm. They just haven't been relevant for a while. I have kept feeding and watering them in the mean time allowing them to take their extending mediation period seriously. They might of even been joined by a third, Keith. I was glad so see them still tied up and enjoying the sense deprivation. Not so much that I had to clean them with a couple of buckets of cold water as they were sat in a puddle of their own excretions. But their usefulness had become a new cog as my plan developed. I removed their headphones.

'Ah Twiddledee and Twiddledum. Or the drug dealer and rapist. Parasites and totally unrequired. Do you know what Vlad the Impaler and the Druids had in common? Hm? What about their sense of power from sacrifice? Just imagine the Otterman hordes stopping in their tracks upon seeing a hundred thousand enemies impaled on Romania's border. You too can also serve through sacrifice yes?'

Like a fine wine I would leave them a further day to ferment upon my proposal. Not that they had a choice! Unlike the others whose lives they had polluted.

As the thunderous clouds part and a shaft of light shines upon me I reached up to the heavens expelling lightning from my fingertips.

'Exodus!!'

Exodus from this planet, Exodus from those encouraging our extinction, Exodus from the species' blinkers.

My visions were becoming exponentially vivid as time became increasing restricted.

It has been sometime since I had an encounter with Anna, however now was the time to renew our acquaintance as her role called forth. Perhaps a disciple to spread my word? Once more I paid homage to her seductive nature upon arrival however something seemed different.

'Do you believe in Gaia?' She asked.

'Sorry?' I replied as I didn't realize this revolutionist had deeper aspects to her aims.

'Gaia, Goddess Earth. Or Gaia concept as a super organism that self regulates? It is alive, yes?'

'I have thought about it.'

'Well, she is alive and we are the microbes or the virus that is out of balance with her. Maybe as an infestation like parasites.'

'Totally agree.'

'What do you think we should do about it?'

'I aim to save life down here'.

'Down here?'

'Yes, on Earth'

'And how can you do this?'

'By initiating the antidote and restoring the balance.' I proposed.

'The antidote? Perhaps you should meet my friends?'

And then I thought to myself, why begin a movement when they already exist. I just need to hijack one and give them a gentle push.

In the meantime I had my two volunteers and like a terrorist's video they would act as my initial sword tip. Even if this might come across as words spoken by those under duress.

'Being the scum of the world, we do not deserve either your respect or attention. We have been granted the right to possess the true purpose. To champion your existence.' Advised Vince.

'As we stand at the gates our wilful self sacrifice is a message to you all.' Darren added.

'There are those who make a difference. And those who choose to hinder them.'

'Let our act be a threat to the hordes who are suffocating the evolution of mankind.'

'Let our act be your inspiration and guidance.'

'And to those who stunt our species future. Let this be the fear that guides you.'

And with a spot of green screen and some editing wizardry zoom out to present them within the torso of a burning Wickerman. How apt I thought to myself that this image like the druids would ward off evil wrong doers. Although I would like this to be real, perhaps burning outside the House of Commons, I am not set up to perform such a publicity stunt nor do I intend to become that which I'm setting out to eradicate. So naturally I released them back into their natural environment minus their clothes. And all once more with the help of Farmer Tyler's tranquilliser gun must add!

Time soon came around when Anna introduced me to her 'associates.' Within this darken meeting room resided a group of very mature subjects. I thought are they contemporary elders as if from a Greek myth. A large monitor hung behind them with a PC on the table. I was comforted in the knowledge I had come prepared. I wasn't sure who was recruiting who as it seemed like something one would witness during a backroom encounter during the Cold War.

Anna introduced me. 'This is Jason. He's the one.' Hardly Neo from The Matrix I thought as my suspicions began to simmer.

'Anna has told us about you. I'm Monique. My colleagues are George, Barbara, Friedrich and Betty.'

Frankly they could have been 'The Jackson 5' as I didn't believe those in such high ranking covert positions would ever divulge any true information to a possible scapegoat. I basically thought they were New Age Druids with delusions of grandeur. Lets see how this plays out anyway I considered.

'Why are you here?' George enquired in an philosophical manner as he looked down his glasses at me.

'Are you of Mayan descent?' Barbara asked as if distant.

'Hi. And what is it you all do? Druids?' Without sounding like their sacrificial lamb as this appeared as an initial interrogation rather than introduction.

'We aim to solve the problems of the world. We are influential.' Friedrich said seeming more accommodating than his motley crew.

'We are The Guardians of Gaia.' Pronounced Anna.

'Ah, right?'

'Tell me Jason, what is the purpose of world domination? What do you know of the grand conspiracy?' George enquired.

'I only see what is necessary.'

'Are you blinkered? What is the psychology to possess and control it all?' Friedrich returned with.

'Maybe the product of a mistreated childhood?'

'Survival maybe?' Said Friedrich

'Maybe greed as an addiction. Ego?'

'And are you the cure for this?' George responded.

'I see it like a virus.'

'Stemming from?' Monique asked in a curious fashion like a sales person funnels you towards their conclusions.

'Us. There is too much demand and not enough supply to sustain a survivable balance. Or more to the point, excessive demands. People are unwilling to sacrifice that which they do not need. Therefore greed is our virus.'

'Maybe the Egyptians already knew this.' Barbara added.

'Tell them about your idea, Jason.' Anna enthusiastically demanded.

'I don't wish to upset you. But you hardly seem reactionary. How are you going to help?'

'Go on, Jason.' Anna enthusiastically encouraged.

In the back of my mind I was reluctant to trust them. I didn't want to be seen as an article of ridicule nor have my plans scuppered. These people might even be representatives of those I wished to condemn and therefore I could be cutting my own throat. It was then I remembered the stepping stones and took a leap of faith. I wasn't destined to walk away from a fate.

'Yes boy, spit it out.' George demanded.

'Think of us as your Argonauts young Jason.' Barbara kindly suggested.

And with baited breath I spoke my mind and divulged my theory.

'A reduction of numbers to balance the equation. I don't just mean a cull, more of a refinement of our species. An efficient species is required.'

'A war of attrition? Perhaps the wars, famine, disease and environmental disasters aren't enough and target the wrong people? What do you propose? Engineer a religion? Construct a belief system? If we have faith in you then our network and influence could be your spear tip.' Friedrich responded.

'Well, my inclinations are more towards John Locke.'

'King Charles II political opponent? 'The pen is mightier than the sword' Wrote the the Two Treaties of Government that became the founding philosophy for the Americans. Life, liberty, freedom etc? Is this what you mean?' George questioned.

'Well that's a great cover for the rampage of global cultural imperialism. God bless the capitalist Americans!' Barbara mocked.

'Yes but, considered as the most dangerous man in history. The most heroic. A menace to tyrants and a liberator of generations.'

'And your vision? Are you dangerous?' Friedrich added with haste.

'Our lifeboat needs shoring up. And supplies are being misappropriated.'

I took out my flash drive containing my preplanned lecture with images of global pollution and brought this up onto their screen.

'I believe greed is the inherit crime of our species. As people won't change, we have to look at the problem from another angle. Survival is simply a case of mathematics. Take the total tonnage by greenhouse gases to a catastrophic point of non reversible climate change return and minus the point where it is sustainable and where future improvement if feasible. Then if taking the average global count 10 tones of green house gases created as per person as global annual average. Then remove the excessive people given there are currently a world population of 8 billion. And hopefully there is our answer. I worked it out to be 800 million. Otherwise stop using fossil fuels which doesn't seem to be feasible at this point. Look this is pollution globally during international lock down. See, this is now. We haven't learned from Gaia's pandemic antibodies.'

'And those remaining? Should they continue with their carbon abuse? Hardley acceptable I think. It makes no sense.' Friedrich pointed out.

'Yes absolutely right. Simply an initial target. Those remaining are The Chosen. A mindset beyond abuse. A beginning. Otherwise maybe the concept of carbon rationing?'

'And how do you propose this cull to begin?' George said in a better manner.

'It's neither a new or original concept. It isn't a cull. It's a revolution.'

'What is your strategy?' Asked Friedrich.

'We need to convince our army, the people. Hearts and minds. We will raise our army from the masses. Remove their blinkers and support their braveness in conviction. Initially though, how do you tell the tribal leader that the God of Fire doesn't exist and that the Earth is round? We show them. A microcosm. A fuse.'

'Viva la revolution!' Monique cheered.

Prior to the meeting with the 'Elders', I had already developed a strategy. I used Mary as my initial sounding board.

'Mary, having experience from a darker place, where do you think the world would be without drugs?'

'That isn't the only thing we are polluted with.'

'That's not what I meant. But it's a start. Its consequence. Those who suffer and those who live in fear. More to the point, those who profit through the enslavement of others. The ivy is suffocating us, yes?' It seemed like I too was now funnelling like a salesperson or a con-man.

'And how do you see this being solved?' Mary replied to a very complex concept.

'Simple. Non-compliance. Gandhi's methods of gaining independence from the British.'

And donning my robes I would once more confront the public with my mighty words of wisdom.

'Turn your backs on tyranny! Non-compliance! We will no longer suffer their abuse of our species! Be free to live. Join the Exodus!! Turn your backs on tyranny! Free our species!'

I would conclude my final speech by pointing out the accused. A gang of hoodlums and trust they would feel our wrath! And with a breath later I would lie upon the grass to feel the Earth's movement whilst getting lost in the clouds above, attempting a connection with Gaia. As I lie here I ask myself whether these are my acts or whether fate is steering me and whether all this has already happened?

And o' where is my burning bush?

8.

THE PLAN.

I felt like a leader announcing his battle-plan to his subjects. Could the 'Elders' really become my disciples? Could their 'influence' spread the word of I?

'I like to refer to it as The Civil Preservation Act. Essentially to purify the species whilst reduce its hindrances. Essentially for those who care not for the world and its species enhancement have no place here.' I advised them.

'Where do we begin?' Asked Anna.

'Initially, I thought about legalising euthanasia. Those who wish to go, let them. And then,'

'The death sentence? Murderers, paedos, drug dealers, human traffickers, slave owners?' Monique interrupter with enthusiasm.

'Precisely.'

'Will this be enough?' George queried.

'Our acts will be a microcosm. A righteous contagion spreading across the globe as a survival pandemic.'

'You and who's army?' Friedrich gently enquired.

'Like John Locke, this is a battle for hearts and minds and the media will be our swords. But unlike the media our acts will not act as entertainment. Where the audience have become immune. There are more of us than them. We fight with the philosophy of Gandhi. Non-compliance. We remove the demand and cultivate new ideals. Those who continue in their crimes will be outcast. They become unnecessary.

Barbara stood tall. 'We will storm the Bastille using its own guards!'

Joined by Friedrich, 'Where the fools imprisoned the wise!'

'Yes, a reversal of the dictators structure. Free the opposition! Champion the intelligent!' Added George.

In the back of my mind, I heard Mary's voice of reason, 'Isn't this going down the path of the dictators death lists? Eugenics? Ethnic cleansing, genocide?'

I climbed onto the table like a leader above his piers. 'No. This is a rebellion against those who choose to murder our futures. Our future selves will cease to exist otherwise. The Civil Preservation Act makes no enemy of the state, race, creed or sex. Only enemies against our evolution!'

Again I heard Mary's voice. 'What makes you different from those already committing such acts?'

'For I have been universally chosen!!'

And with that I felt the room light flicker as my words, my destiny struck like a bolt of lightning as I saw the Wickerman burning as a beacon of hope to us all and justice to those who refused to become enlightened.

With all the twines becoming a reality I was in good spirits. The political agenda was set in motion as soon would be my rocket.

'It is beautiful. Art.' Mary said as if admiring a Rembrandt.

'Like every brush stroke, each component has an essential purpose and is integral for the larger masterpiece.'

'And how is it going?'

'Sadly man is not an Octopus. Despite all my efforts there is only so much I can achieve with one set of hands and one brain.'

'Simple. You need more brains and more hands!'

'Although there is an element of secrecy, it's not through lack of trying. Like when Alan Turin, the inventor of the computer, posted a competition to find the right minds. I too posted an ad, 'Can Superman fly?'

'Interesting. Prove the physics and biology yes? Discover those with the imagination, will and ability to engineer.'

'Something like that.'

'Any response?'

'None.'

'Hmm. Well just off the top of my head. Maybe it's simply a perspective of escape velocity. He doesn't have to have the thrust like a rocket, just lighter than his environment and gravity? Perhaps a body that constitutes an electromagnetic field. Displacement? Or Krypton, being larger, it has greater gravity so on Earth like us on the Moon, he would float. Jason, you're not the only nerd in the village!'

Forever resurrecting me from the potential of despair, she ruffled my hair like a playful sister before leaving the lab.

Admiring the rocket and with a sense of satisfaction my thoughts drifted to my father as I remember us sat by the water's edge on the shore. He placed a note in a bottle that simply read: BE MORE.

'What do you think is the probability of anyone ever receiving this? Let alone it having any effect?' Asked Dad.

And with that he tossed it as far as he could into the sea.

'I imagine a rescue or a record of existence. Perhaps hope? Dad? Would it work better if the tide was going out?'

'Well done son.'

With every lesson Dad taught me I believe he was either preparing me for my destiny or permitting the possibility to complete that which he wasn't in a position to do.

I slept very little with the constant ideas surfacing. Mary was still awake and my pillow talk was not that of your stereotypical couple.

'Do you believe in global warning?' I asked openly.

'Yes. All created from our greed.'

'Maybe so. We are certainly not helping. Did you know the ice caps on Mars are melting? Humans can't be at fault for this.'

'The sun is getting hotter.'

'Yes, and increasingly reactive.'

'So what does this mean?'

'Outside of a stars natural life, there is a suggestion that our solar system is passing through a highly energized cloud fuelling the suns activity.'

'We have no choice then.'

'I believe we only have to choose to evolve and move on. We could otherwise descend underground like HG Well's Morlocks. This could only last for a given length of time. Quite simple really, like Occam's Razor we just need to remove distractions to attain our destiny.'

'It is our distractions that make us human.' I imagined she was thinking.

I cannot recall falling to my slumber however I do recall my dreams which I had the understanding of being more. My visions.

I could picture the message 'Be More and The Civil Preservation Act' being advertised on social media, bill boards, the sides of buses, labelled in protests and marketing campaigns. All of which abused and becoming out of context leading to unnecessary unrest.

I imagined a Search & Rescue man dashing through the thick woodland undergrowth reaching a cliff's edge where a man was clinging on for his dear life.

'Tom? Tom Fincher?'

'Help! Over here! Save me!'

The rescue man slowly approaches before calmly sitting.

'As I sit here, I look at you struggling, desperately clinging on. And I think to myself, I remember all those who I didn't reach in time. The lost, the suicidal and the accidental. I remember those I wept for. And then there's you. Who would weep for you I ask myself? Certainly not those whose lives you have destroyed and ofcourse those you potentially could. So I ask you simply, let go. The world truly doesn't need you?'

Tom struggles before loosing his grip and falling to his death.

'Paedo.'

Was this the beginnings of the revolution I thought? Was this the eventualities of my actions? My thoughts drifted to the potential consequent actions of the 'Elders.'

And within the musty, backdrop of a gentleman's club two old men sat on Chesterfield leather wing-back chairs smoking Cuban cigars with their single malt whiskeys.

'And on the other matter George, how is our little project developing?' Asked Sir Robin.

'We have found our Pinocchio. And our campaign is gathering momentum.'

'Good. And out of chaos cometh order. Cometh control.' As smoke billowed from Sir Robin's grimace.

'In fact it is better than planned. He actually believes he is the reincarnation of Moses.'

'Would you believe he's even given us the perfect umbrella. The Civil Preservation Act.' George smugly advised.

'And what about recourse?'

'Laughable, plausible deniability. After all Anna told him we were the 'Guardians of Gaia'. We don't exist.'

They clinked glasses as if striking a deal with an the utter disregard for Project Exodus whilst endeavouring to profiteer.

I had what I presumed to be a final meeting with 'The Guardians of Gaia' even though I remaining distrustful of their true intentions.

'How will all this take place?' I asked.

'People power. Engage their will to survive against oppression.' George responded.

'Let them see their oppressors.' Monique advised in a somewhat unconvincing radical manner.

'Everyman hath a right to punish the offender, and be executioner of the law of nature.' George paraphrased.

'James Locke?' I believed.

''The quest is righteous and there is no option.' Friedrich affirmed.

''They say we are governed by the choices that are presented to us and not those of our own making. Therefore we are susceptible to that which is presented.' Monique quite rightly pointed out.

'And utilising the algorithms that steer our presented choices, we will direct your message to those who count.' George seemed to be the real man of action rather than theorists.

'And then?'

'Quite simply, we give it a little push!' Responded Friedrich optimistically.

Initially unconvinced of their methods, on seeing the news over the following week I wasn't sure how far the Guardian's influence reached.

'In an unforeseen change of circumstances the accused serial child rapist and murderer, Thomas Hemin has walked free from court on a technicality. Justice has been called into question and there are fears of public repercussions.' The News Reader advised.

It was only a matter of time before faith would be lost in the justice system and could give rise to vigilantism. Just imagine the general suspicion parents would have for those around their children. What would be the outcome when the pride of lions are faced with a threat?

I stand alone bearing nothing but the skin that wraps me. Shouting at the heavens abovc.

'Was it my fault? Did I kill them? Was my destiny to be the end of theirs?

'Let them all burn?'

'Crack whore!' Why was I spared? I shouldn't be here. It's all my fault. They shouldn't of been sacrificed for me. They didn't deserve this. I blame you God! Look what you have done!

Lightning barrels across the night's sky as I demanded answers. Is it I who became the threat to the lion's pride? Was it I who became the cuckoo that destroyed my parent's nest and consequently to all of those who share this planet and their fates? Does this world need me? Could doubt be my true enemy?

9.

ENTROPY, THE SINGULARITY AND INFINITY

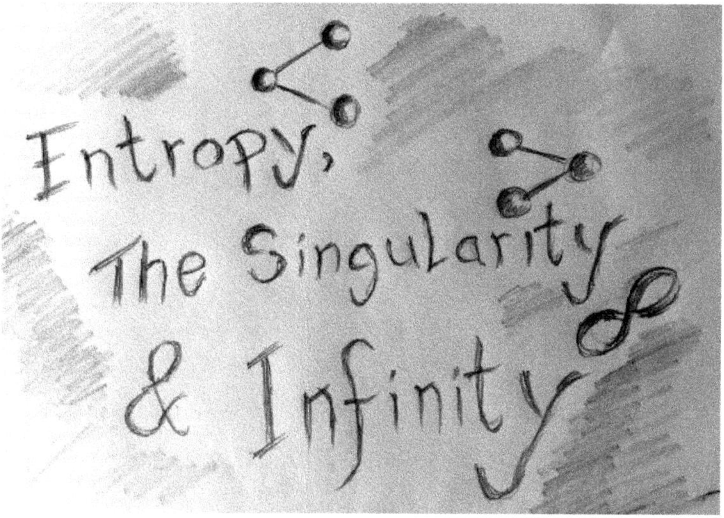

It is believed that in maths there are only 3 true numbers. 0, 1 and infinity. Nothing, something and everything.

Entropy:

Life restoring to a natural state of chaos.

I must walk the path I preach leading by example. Compassion is the key I tell myself venturing into a degraded urban slum in search of those lost and trapped. Do all of the blind hide behind hoodies?

'What ya got?' I asked a young adult.

'FXXk off Grandad.'

'I'm serious. What ya selling?'

'Piss off copper.'

'I've got cash. You got ganga? coke? meth? heroine? I've got a party.'

'Might know someone who can hook you up.'

'Where would you be without me?'

'What?'

'If there was no demand, where would you be? If I turn my back on you, if we all turn our backs on you, where would you be?'

I'm not certain whether he shared my perspective of a uber-wealthy Colombian Drug Barron in his luxury mansion to the smugglers, dealers and factories producing their products, to the fields harvesting the ingredients to the street addicts and consequent violence that poverty and greed battle with. Further more like the tributaries of a river the money that flows from the street to the government that denies its collections. Maybe even the sponsorship of power struggles internationally. Did this youth share such visions? Could he turn his back on this wicked world?

'And the person you answer to. And their next? Where would you all be? If we all turn our backs on you? Like lemmings on a cliff's edge? Would the world still turn without you? Would the gene pool be aided without you all?' I asked.

Seeing me as a threat, this dealer pulls out a blade. I wished for the appearance of a celebratory marching brass band with marionettes twirling their batons backlit with a mighty firework display.

'And with your choice made. We celebrate your sacrifice. Death to those who dilute our gene pool!'

Upon the mount I give my final internet sermon.

'People of law enforcement stand aside and let justice prevail. Wardens throw away your keys and let them rot. Medics make your choices to those who deserve your aid whilst the transition takes place. Criminals against survival find your cliffs. For we will no longer suffer your tyranny. To those who share a greater vision, exile our enemies! They will rot without us. They will become extinct! Without them our species will only benefit. Join the Exodus. Become what your destined to be.'

We the many, march banners held high through Whitehall to Westminster. Sporting the costumes of superheroes, Batman, Wonder Woman, Superman and The Vision just mention a few. With their leader as Moses being their tip of their spear, their saviour to confront the Otterman hordes. This is our final stand!

'As protests have turned to violence, the police struggle to contain the rioters who have claimed their actions in the name of vigilante group EXODUS.' Reported the BBC.

'We will no longer suffer the tyranny of those who seek to destroy our future!' Shouted Batman.

With Bruce Springsteen's 'Dancing in the Dark' resonating through my head I questioned the forthcoming direction my quest had taken. Everything appeared in slow motion as the rioters parted like the Dead Sea upon my approach. The villains had become the prey upon the serge of the vigilantes bearing burning torches. Brutal beatings and hangings seemed common place as the Riot Police stood back. And firebombs were employed against the articles of criminal profiteering. No law abiding property was touched.

'Let them burn!' I heard bellowed amongst the mobs anger.

It seemed like history echoed the French or Russian Revolutions where the hierarchy were overturned by the proletariat.

A crack house door is nailed shut and a black cross is sprayed on it to symbolise that which plagued us. It then lit as if a purge has commenced.

'This is for all those lives you've destroyed!'

'Death to drug dealers!'

'Death to scum!!' The angry horde hollowed aloud!

The screams of the occupants become haunting. This was not my design for they are simply the victims of others. This was not non-compliance.

The media revelled with their headlines as the mass hysteria had spread like an epidemic. I could imagine the over dramatised American reporting with all its regalia.

'With the current upheaval in the UK overspilling here our panel of guests will discuss the Righteousness of the Riots and whether Vigilantism can be Victorious? Joining us in the studio we have guests from the Republican Senate, a Humans Rights Lawyer and a member of the newly formed American faction of Exodus. We demand answers! Where will this revolution end? Is this the backhanded work of the Commies? Or is this the beginning of a New World Order?'

With the cindering remains from the previous night's battle all seemed serene. This time it was The Verve, 'Bitter Sweet Symphony' that became my soundtrack to the empty streets with the burnt out cars and properties. I thought about the hierarchy of command is not held with the righteous, its origins lied with the savage.

Afterall, prior to government, there was the inbreeding of Royals wishfully designed to become higher human beings. Before pronouncing theirselves as kings they were War Lords and prior to this barbarians. The survival of the fittest. Intelligence should become the new strength rather than might. I somehow believe this would never become a reality as it goes against nature's rules for survival. It might be interesting if barbarians became extinct. One shouldn't wage war with the next, I would hope. Would our enemies share such sentiments? If you can't trade then you take yes? No! As Gandhi once put it, 'An eye for an eye leaves the world blind.' Non-compliance. Remove the demand and the fear will become extinct. That is was my intention. Not this however, as far as cause and effect is concerned, out of chaos I have influenced a pure vision. Being like the sure shot from a Mongolian Foot Archer! A singularity and hope for beyond.

My blindfold was removed and I was bound to a chair being held in the barn where my social experiments once commenced with Tweedledee and Tweedledum.

A silhouetted figure looms out of the darkness.

'Turn you back on tyranny? Without tyranny there is no struggle. Without a struggle there is no evolution, there is no life. It is a necessity. 8 Billion Beautiful Brains? They have the choice and yet the beast is still being fed regardless of consequence and inevitability. Or perhaps a greater vision is simply futile.'

Was this my PE teacher or was it one of the Guardians?

A lamb is brought forth. Is this sacrificial? Am I sacrificial or is this penance for acts against rapists?

Outside the House of Commons Sir Robin MP was caught before entering the building.

'Sir Robin, is this not the beginning of the end for our justice system? And how do we prevent its powers from being abused if due process is forsaken?' Asked the TV News Reporter.

'We can only condemn the current rioting however it supports the feeling and want of our nation towards the need of The Civil Preservation Bill.' Responded Sir Robin before escaping.

Returning to my house I found Mary looking somewhat distant, sat staring out the window with an open laptop beside her.

'Are you OK?'

'They're dead...'

'Who?'

'The dealers, the rapists, the scum.'

'Then why are you shedding tears?'

'Have you seen this?'

It appears Mary has witnessed the confession of Vince and Darren that has gone viral after their bodies were discovered, according to a news stream she was watching.

'And?' I asked.

'And?' Mary echoed as if I was ignorant.

'I don't understand. Aren't you pleased? You are safe. You are free.'

'Free? What is the world about to become?' Mary asked rhetorically.

'Isn't this what you want?'

'Vigilantism, anarchy & chaos?'

'Hey, cheer up life will be better now.'

'Jason, you live in a totally different world from the rest of us. There is no black and white. The world is not binary.'

'Ever heard of the 'Guardians of Gaia?'

'What?'

'They believe in me, my message and our future survival.'

'Do you know what you sound like?'

'They believe I am the one. And I always knew it.'

'Are you their puppet? Are you getting fisted? Who are they? Do you really know Jason?'

'The future. They recognize me as a modern day Moses.'

'The only thing you have in common with Moses is you have downloaded from the Cloud to your Tablet! You are but a naive innocent kid Jason. What do you know of the real world? Have all your followers, customs & speeches deluded you? Like my father?'

'I don't understand?'

'And that is the problem! Isn't it! Cause and effect. Ask yourself, what is it they want? Did this ever cross your mind? Are they a cult? Apocalyptic? Or profiteering? Jason, we are ruled by parasitical psychopaths who plunge us into war, manipulate us against each other, and flood our minds with fear, hate, bigotry and ignorance with every change they get. Is this them? Does this sound familiar?'

Ofcourse Mary was right, she was rarely wrong.

Although I had been blindfolded when meeting with the 'Guardians of Gaia', I wasn't foolish and knew where they were based. I ventured to seek the truth behind their motives. I couldn't see the others only George as I sneaked into the building. And there he was sat at his desk in a dimly lit room.

'Every revolution has its leader? Don't you mean a puppet? What do you profit from my acts?'

He laughed as if the 'game' was up.

'Profit? You are but a tiny element in the larger experiment dear boy. However once a reaction has occurred there is no longer a need for the catalyst!'

George lifts his concealed revolver from the desk draw. I can't confirm whether time slowed as I closed my eyes and anticipated the inevitable.

BANG!

I felt no pain. Was this the afterlife I asked? It couldn't be as my destiny wasn't forfilled. I wasn't due the Reaper's visit yet I told myself. And with a loud thud, I opened my eyes to see George's lifeless body fall against the desk. His blood pooling across his paperwork whilst his brains spattered over a newspaper featuring the headlines from Exodus.

Anna stepped forward from the darkness blowing the smoke from the barrel of her pistol like a proud western gun slinger.

'Like he said. Once the reaction has taken place, there is no further need for the catalyst.'

She smiled before leaving. And that was the last I ever saw of her.

'The body of the controversial industrialist George Donestez has been discovered dead in his London offices. Police are questioning a woman in her mid-thirties. The motives have been suggested as politically motivated as activists from 'Exodus' have claimed responsibility.' A News Reader announced.

'Is this related to you? Do you know what you've done? This is not 'non-compliance'. This is not Gandhi! Do you have blood on your hands?' Mary demanded!

'I've been hi-jacked. The concept has taken on its own life. It's trying to save our futures by extinguishing the parasites that blind our future selves.'

'And what if it doesn't work? Have you considered the consequences if you actions spread?'

'That's what I'm banking on.'

'Have you considered what we see as crime in other cultures it is simply survival. Where are the borders for morals?'

'I know it doesn't make it right but the same argument still stands.'

'And what about natural attrition? Nature has a balance between its predators and worker ants. Outcasts become our enemies.'

'I don't understand you. Why should we live in fear? We have no option. Can't you see this?'

'Not every revolution is successful.' She advised.

'Then the opposite approach is required. Reverse psychology. If you want to seize their attention to 'Save The Badger' then you advertise a cull. How about we champion a campaign where greed is good? Lavishing in excess where more is better. Bigger cars, bigger houses, gluttony! Perhaps with the motto:

'LIVE FAST DIE YOUNG FOR EXTINCTION IS INEVITABLE.'

Such outlandish vulgar philosophies leading to disgust if they fail to listen to, 'There are more of us than them. Non-compliance will drive our persecutors into extinction.'

'Mary, what do you think? Or would the blinkered remain resigned to this concept without further thought?'

As a boy I recall seeing the soothsayer, the 11th Doctor for a final time whilst all else passed by like ghosts in the mist.

'They have been infected by delusion. It has become a pandemic. They know their fate. Ignorance is bliss. Close your eyes and the monster will disappear. Well, Jason it's your fate to change theirs. Lead those who wish to 'Be More.' The rest can remain wilfully blinkered.' Advised Matt Smith's doppelganger.

The Singularity.

My visions of the steeping stones crossing the river shone bright.

'With every step leads to the next. With faith and destiny aside. Am I being delusional? If they could see what I see, would a revolution occur? What if they new it was the basis for a cull? Exodus? Earth's population being 8 billion, 800 million would have to be sacrificed. The remainder could still enjoy their carbon expending comforts there after. Otherwise could we all follow a concept of carbon rationing? Where commercial gain was deemed to be no longer of any profit for our species' survival? How would this wash with the hierarchy? And what about the external plan? Now that is a must. And I would regret nothing. However, could my efforts result in World War 3? The Nuclear Apocalypse? If the Rocketoon was taken by the jet steam over paranoid territories how would they react? Who's finger would press that big RED BUTTON? The Chinese, the Americans, the North Koreans, The Russians or us? Perhaps some doors should never be opened? And then I ask myself is there an alternative?

I dreamt of the payload drifting through space awaiting its opportunity to leap-frog onwards, continually evolving to survive.

Infinity.

I have a Future's Dream of a large clean building set in the middle of a world which has come to its senses. In the foray sits those who can contribute more with a large screen before them repeating a message to the masses.

We have limited time here.
All life evolved from a single cell.
Let life evolve from you.
Live Forever can launch your DNA into space aboard our rocket the MESOPOTAMIA.
Together we can seed the universe.
Book your space today.
Don't get left behind!
Panspermia.

The end logo depicts us leap frogging onward between the worlds underlined with the words: Ingenio Legatum (Genius Legacy).

'Please this way Mr Sage.' Leads the concierge.

'What is this? Live Forever?' Mr Sage innocently asks.

She leads him to an area such as Alice was led through the looking glass.

'Simply a doorway. Hope. We believe Superman can fly. And so do you. Pick a door.'

There are 3 DOORS. Mr Sage stands before them. They are simply numbered.

'Which one?' He inquires.

'Well door one will, with your help discover memory to hereditary instinct. Two, is creating the survivable transient form leaving three, Transportation of the form. Pick.'

It is at this point the later uplifting part from Queen's song, 'Who wants to live forever' celebrates our potential. And the initial success of a balloon launch commences being observed by myself holding hands with my saviour Mary who is bearing our child.

'Fingers crossed, ignition, the burn, avoid orbital debris, satellites, the ISS and ofcourse escape gravity!'

Is there anything else we can hope for being on the outer regions of a galaxy spinning beyond a black hole?

With a kiss upon my brow, Mary brings a calm reality to my tormented slumber.

'Wake up Jason.' She asks with a delightful smile.

I thought my awakening would be a future self evolved as a cephalopod with an enlarged frontal lobe aboard a spaceship releasing seeds to a planet below. As the capsule strikes the planet's water mass the dividing of the cell commences.

I was in reality residing within the hospital amongst the books, my sketches, my paintings and my plans that aided my mental recovery. Was I a victim of Delusional Syndrome of Predetermination? Was I misidentifying the signs? In reality, were the signs of any true relevance when addressing the demands placed on us all?

Mary passes my father's journal titled 'Ingenio Legatum.'

'I found it, it's yours.'

And within it's first page I found a note.

For my son, and the lineage he saves within us all.
Dad X

It's all a matter of cause and effect. Eventualities. To avoid my future self's mistakes I examined the possibilities here. And all these visions and plans are purely a stepping stone beyond my personal exile. If one perceives their acts as righteous and necessary then I can only let pure hope be the inspiration to guide us. Let my future words and actions resonate through eternity. 8 Billion Beautiful Brains. Let us become everything. Let us 'Be More.' We owe our future selves this legacy.

And with this I left to begin what needs to be done.

Next episode:
Eventualities –

The truth lies within the practice of reality.

www.ingramcontent.com/pod-product-compliance
Ingram Content Group UK Ltd.
Pitfield, Milton Keynes, MK11 3LW, UK
UKHW021855150925
462938UK00004B/27

9 798231 821198